THINGS WE DO WHEN
no one IS WATCHING

Also by Philip Gerard

Fiction

The Dark of the Island
Desert Kill
Cape Fear Rising
Hatteras Light

Nonfiction

Down the Wild Cape Fear:
    A River Journey Through the Heart of North Carolina
The Patron Saint of Dreams (essays)
Secret Soldiers—The Story of World War II's Heroic Army of Deception
Writing Creative Nonfiction (ed. with Carolyn Forché)
Creative Nonfiction—Researching and Crafting Stories of Real Life
Brilliant Passage . . . a schooning memoir
The Art of Creative Research: A Field Guide for Writers

THINGS WE DO WHEN
no one IS WATCHING

stories

Philip Gerard

BkMk Press
University of Missouri-Kansas City
www.umkc.edu/bkmk

BkMk Press
University of Missouri-Kansas City
5101 Rockhill Road
Kansas City, MO 64110
www.umkc.edu/bkmk

Executive Editor: Robert Stewart
Managing Editor: Ben Furnish
Assistant Managing Editor: Cynthia Beard

Cover art: Doug Hansen

BkMk Press thanks the Miller-Mellor Foundation for its support.

BkMk Press also thanks Dana Sanginari, Barbara Magiera, Serena Dobson, Josiah Pabst, McKensie Callahan, and Thea Voutiritsas.

Library of Congress Cataloging-in-Publication Data

Names: Gerard, Philip, author.
Title: The things we do when no one is watching : short fiction / by Philip Gerard.
Description: Kansas City, MO : BkMk Press, 2017.
Identifiers: LCCN 2017023682 | ISBN 9781943491094 (alk. paper)
Classification: LCC PS3557.E635 A6 2017 | DDC 813/.54--dc23 LC record available at https://lccn.loc.gov/2017023682

ISBN: 978-1-943491-09-4

Contents

Night Camp 9

Gloriana 19

Stepping Into Flight 29

Miracle Boy 37

Ace 51

O Canada 69

The Circus Train 81

Death by Reputation 93

Flexible Flyer 109

This Is the Story I Want To Tell 123

Davey Terwilliger 141

The Man Who Fell Out of the Sky 145

In Dreams Begin 157

Things We Do When No One Is Watching 163

Acknowledgments

"Night Camp" *The Green Mountains Review*

"Flexible Flyer" *North Carolina Literary Review*

"Gloriana," "Miracle Boy" *New Letters*

"Ace" *The Greensboro Review*

"O Canada" *Cold Mountain Review*

"The Circus Train" *Iron Horse Literary Review*

"Death by Reputation" (*New England Review/ Bread Loaf Quarterly*, reprinted in *This Is Where We Live* (University of North Carolina Press)

"Stepping into Flight" *Carolina Style*

"This Is the Story I Want To Tell" *Water-Stone Review*

"Davey Terwilliger" *Long Story Short* (University of North Carolina Press)

"The Man Who Fell Out of the Sky" *Controlled Burn, a North Woods Literary Journal*

"In Dreams Begin" *The Raleigh News & Observer*

For all my teachers—with gratitude

Night Camp

It was a strange place, made stranger by the little campers who inhabited it for six weeks every summer. I came there for a job between college terms, answering an ad in the student union, and spent just that single haunting season there.

Night Camp, as we called it, had an Indian name I have long forgotten. But clear in my mind even now are the line of stilted cabins on the narrow bench of land between the lake and Kanatauka Ridge, the swale of bright green meadow scooped out of the hills where the riding stables and pony ring stood, and the red-clay scar of a trail that meandered from the meadow up through the folded hills and then crossed the saddle of the ridgeline before descending through a scrub forest and looping back to the cabins.

There was something beautifully contained about it, though the north country sprawled around it wild and rugged for a hundred miles in any direction. To the east, the ridge and hills bunkered the sky; to the south, a narrow defile ran into the pony meadow. North led past the cabins and through a winding wooded dirt track for miles to the state highway, and of course the western edge of the place dissolved into the lake. The constant prevailing breeze rasped across the water in a perpetual restless sigh, and the water shone like a spread of jewels on velvet—for we always saw it at night, and what we were seeing was starlight spangling the surface of the water.

Darkness—that was the point. Rakes, the head counselor, explained it to me that first afternoon. These were kids who couldn't stand the daytime. They had sensitive eyes, allergies to sunlight, porcelain-fair skin prone to cancer. A few were terribly disfigured in ways the surgeons could not fix: Calvin had a face that was half blond and freckled, with one bright blue eye, and half that was a rough blue-scarlet patch with an eye socket sewn shut—he had been burned almost to death in his crib. Libby was a tiny girl of nine or ten with long brown hair which she never wore in pigtails, because then you could see her missing right ear.

They also had problems of a more metaphorical nature—if that is the word. Silvio, a dark-eyed kid with a bowl of flat-black hair, was pathologically shy. He slept under his bunk and often wore a kerchief mask like an Old West stagecoach robber.

Trina hid behind aliases—it's hard to remember what she looked like, because almost every day she changed her appearance. One day she was a blonde with a ready smile, the next she turned into a brooding redhead with painted eyes. She could make herself seem tall and willowy or squat and plump. She even changed her name. "I'm Samantha," she would insist one day, and the next would scold me for calling her Samantha. "Don't you recognize me? I'm Lexie!"

I say "day," but it was always night. That was the point.

My first night, I stumbled around barking my shins on footlockers and found the bathrooms only by the weak glow of the single forty-watt bulb mounted in a shade above the doorway. All lighting was subdued at Night Camp, and whenever possible it was turned off completely.

The kids, though, glided around completely at ease. It dawned on me almost immediately that these were kids who had drifted through their families' homes like ghosts all their lives, navigating between the sharp edges of tables and stepping over sleeping dogs without waking them, all completely silently. They were children of the darkness, at home in the shadows, safely hidden from—what?

I didn't know exactly.

That was the strangest thing about Night Camp, how completely silent it was. Most summer camps are raucous mobs of shouting and singing and screaming laughter and cheers, but not Night Camp. Have you ever watched a game of slow-pitch softball played under a full moon in absolute silence? The 12-inch ball arcing in from the pitcher's hand fat as a pumpkin, and the only sound the dead thump of the bat against it and the grunting of the kid sprinting to first base? Then you hear the *fop* of the ball in bare hands and maybe the base runner kicking dirt off his sneakers, and it all starts again. There is no patter. Nobody cheers or boos. And when the game is over everyone seems to know it and simply walks dutifully off the field, like workers after a shift at the factory, and carefully stows the bats and balls in the canvas gear bag.

We had no campfires. You would think we had campfires every night, but the night was a soothing pool of blind solace. Not just the condition of the planet that has for a few hours turned its face away from the sun, but a place all its own, a hole in time where it was possible to be yourself and swim in the darkness as in a refreshing breeze.

Some nights, the campers rode ponies. At dawn, the ponies always came back. I was not a riding counselor, and I would watch the line of ponies cross the ridge, distant as toys, and wait for them to return before the light spilled down over the silvering treeline into our hollow of time and space beside the sparkling lake.

Rakes would blow his whistle—not a shrill coach's whistle but a wooden whistle that made a soft sound like a bird—*whirr-ree*—and the ponies would perk up their ears and bob their heads and trundle the kids toward the corral. The kids would dismount and file back to their cabins, where I had already lowered all the sleeping blinds.

And in the broad light of day, the place was as deserted as the moon.

Yet it was not silent then. The children did not sleep quietly. I would sit in an Adirondack chair on the saggy porch and listen to their sighs and dreaming voices inside. Silvio, so shy during his waking hours, would laugh and prattle on in Spanish. Calvin, in the next bunk over, would answer him in some language no one else spoke, and in this manner they carried on a conversation only they could comprehend, like improvised music, and only while asleep. Other boys were visited by the same lively dreams, and they spent the day in the darkened cabin cooing and whispering and giggling, all while dead asleep. It might have been a rookery.

I would doze in my chair, sometimes dreaming. Because of the odd nocturnal schedule, I never got a real night's sleep in six weeks. One night a week I was off-duty and could sleep in a special cabin reserved for the counselors, but the rest of the time I caught what sleep I could—an hour here, two hours there—so that the whole six weeks came to seem like its own dream. I was never rested, yet never exhausted. Like the others, I moved slowly, never in a hurry, and after a couple of days relaxed into a near constant state of meditative wakefulness.

My chair had thick sun-bleached blue cushions that fastened over the boards with ties, and I could settle into its arms and wait out the daylight with a novel that never seemed to get anywhere, the story stalled in a salon in St. Petersburg, Napoleon and his Old Guard just beyond the river, the snow gathering in purple mammatus above the Russian steppes, snow sifting down on the lights of Moscow, and that suited me fine.

An hour or so before they woke, the boys would relax into silence. The silence would last only so long, and then I would realize that I had been hearing a soft hum for some minutes before registering it—as regular and unobtrusive as the hum of a refrigerator in a quiet kitchen. The hum would be joined by others at different pitches, atonal but oddly melodic. Not harmony exactly but *harmonious*, so that I would freeze in my chair, let my book close by itself like a spring-loaded door, and simply take in the music of their muted voices the way you turn your face into a soft breeze, just to feel it brush your cheeks.

All at once, as if on signal, the humming would cease, and now I could hear coughing and throats clearing and the first boys thumping out of bed to use the john and get dressed.

In the twilight, they filed out toward the dining hall, and across the camp the other three cabins would release their little people and the four lines would converge in silence on the low-roofed log pavilion for a supper of hot dogs or spaghetti.

The second day, Rakes said, "Whatever happens, don't let yourself fall in love with them. You and I, we can't live where they live." Rakes was short and muscled, nearing forty, and in real life he owned a movie theater in a small town in Vermont, an old-fashioned one-screen house that still showed matinee serials and cartoons on Saturday afternoons. "For a little while maybe, for a few weeks, but in the end, we always leave them in the dark."

Natalia, the slim, dark counselor in Libby and Trina's cabin, nodded soberly and bit her lower lip in a way that made me wonder how much of her life story had happened at night. She and Rakes seemed to share some unspoken bond, the way they would speak with their eyes to one another, as if they had known each other all their lives.

The second night, we worked together. Our kids played Junebug, a game I learned at Night Camp and never heard of anyplace else. One kid is the Junebug. He or she goes off into the woods and hides. The other kids walk slowly into the woods in a scattered group, like infantry advancing into enemy territory. The Junebug comes up behind one and claps her hands close, and now that kid is also a Junebug. The Junebugs stalk the others until all are clapped into Junebugs. The last kid clapped gets to be the new Junebug, and off he or she goes into the woods.

Silvio was a great Junebug. He could move like a shadow through any landscape, invisible and weightless. His feet never crunched on leaves or snapped a twig. He clapped his hands short and sharp as a .22 caliber rifle shot. He was the only one who made the other kids flinch, and whenever he caught one, he smiled, just for a second, a bright flash of teeth and a crinkling of eyes. When he was not a Junebug, he wore a red kerchief over his mouth, and in the moon shadows it looked black.

After we had put our campers to bed for the day, Natalia and I slipped off together to a shady clearing beside the lake. She laced her arms around my neck and we kissed for a while. She was sweet and sad, I thought then and still do, and her kisses were soft and lingering, full of comfort but not passion.

Near the end of my first week, Rakes and I were walking back from the canoe landing. I asked him, "What's your story?"

"I could ask you the same question," he said, as if he knew something secret about me that even I myself did not know. He looped an arm around my bony shoulder and said, "Did you know that when you watch a movie, more than half the time you're watching darkness? Your eye is just playing a trick on your brain. It takes all those still images and makes sense out of them. The screen is light and darkness and then light. Your brain sees only the light."

"That's a good thing," I said.

"Yes," he said. "It's the best thing." That was Rakes all over—he just said things out of the blue and left you to ponder what he meant.

Later, down by the lake, I told this to Natalia. She stared across the wind-chopped water as if watching something far away. "I guess it works that way for some people. Most people."

"Not for you?"

She shook her head gently, smiled a little, as if embarrassed. "No, I don't believe it works that way for me."

"What are you seeing now?" I asked.

She shivered slightly and continued staring. "The dark frames in between, one after another." I held her, and when we kissed, our eyes were closed.

The weeks passed, and Natalia and I had our secrets. We slipped away and spooned under the canoes. We kissed in brief encounters during the moments in between here and there. I cupped her soft little breasts and felt her shiver and squeeze me and breathe hot in my ear. I felt light-headed most of the time, quietly euphoric, seeing things that weren't there in the dark—a wavery wedge of geese crossing the moon, shaggy animals slumping through the brushy woods, the floating ghost of my own mother who had died the year before, mute and afraid, of a disease I couldn't even pronounce. She would visit me in waking dreams, settling on me wordlessly in the darkness, at peace, I think, and I would have her until the light chased her away.

The kids grew stronger. Silvio fell in love with Trina but could never muster the nerve to tell her. So he just followed her around, stopping when she stopped—always a few steps behind her and out of reach, grinning with his eyes over his bandit mask—and she caught on. They were like two young mallards pairing around together, never touching but always quietly absorbed in each other's company.

Calvin made himself an eye patch in leather crafts, and this made him look oddly comic, his single blue eye vivid and electric, and he enjoyed the effect. In the still heart of the summer, when the lake went windless and the surface held a slick scrim of oily dust, Libby cut off her long hair and nobody seemed to even notice the misshapen sickle of white cartilage on her right temple. What was gone was invisible. What was lost had disappeared thoroughly into the night. There was a palpable sense that things were winding down. On the second-to-last evening, we hiked the kids into the pasture to play games they made up and brought them back tired and softened by exercise.

Later that afternoon, while I was napping in my chair and dreaming of Russian soldiers barefoot in the snow, Rakes nudged me awake and hunkered down at my elbow. "There was an—*accident*—a few years ago, maybe you remember it," he said.

It took me a few moments to understand he was talking to me, for he was whispering so softly his voice might have been part of my dream. What in the world was he talking about, and why now?

"It happened up north. A school bus was trapped in a blizzard, completely covered over. It took them almost a week to find it."

I remembered it from the endless TV news loop. I was only a little kid then, riding a school bus for the first time, and it made an impression. It was a hard story to forget, one of those famous stories that happen out in the world and are part of history and make you draw closer to the fire and your own loved ones. "All those kids," I said.

"Forty inches of snow in forty hours," he said. "It covered the windows."

I could see the white snow piling up into darkness, a shade being drawn over their lives.

"They went to sleep, you see, one by one. Just fell asleep." He lost himself in the awful vision for a moment. "Only one kid stayed awake."

"Natalia."

He nodded. In his squinting eyes I recognized a small gratitude for accepting this knowledge.

It should have come as a surprise, but she had already taught me about the dark moments in between the frames of light. Each of the light frames was only a temporary respite from loss. Or maybe the dark frames were the reprieve, a hideout from memory and consciousness. "She'll be taking out the ponies tonight," he said. "There's still enough moon." He paused. "You can come with us if you like."

It was the only time I ever rode the ponies. Natalia led on a yellow pony and the kids followed, the ponies with their heads down, nickering softly as if glad to be out of the corral. I rode behind Silvio, ahead of Calvin, and last of all came Rakes, to make sure nobody got lost or left. It was nothing special, just a slow meander along a well-worn trail. We leaned into the ponies' necks as they plodded uphill out of the treeline and then sat tall along the ridge and felt the ponies' swaying warm bodies falling gently from under us as we descended, and then the ride was over, and the next evening I would kiss Natalia goodbye and leave ahead of the others and always wonder if any of it had ever really happened at all.

But I have a postcard from Rakes to prove it, in a fashion. The picture on the front shows an old-fashioned movie-house with a brick facade, and spelled out in backlit letters on the marquee is a movie called *Night Camp*.

It happened in Vermont, the blizzard. A long time later, I found a newspaper clipping. It names the town, the same one where Rakes operated the Cucalorus Theater and worked a second job as a school-bus driver for the county. He was only twenty-five, barely older than I was at Night Camp, when he slewed the yellow bus into a deep ravine and the whiteout turned into frigid darkness for nearly a week, and he waited for rescue with all those children.

It has been thirty years now since I have stepped foot in that part of the world, and I doubt I could even find it on a real map. Natalia and I never did more than kiss and hold each other, in daylight and darkness. It was for the best. When I drove the rutted track out of Night Camp, I was leaving for my senior year at the university. The bug-spotted headlights of my old Ford truck splashed across the trees, throwing murky light onto the road ahead. I lurched around a bend, and there was Silvio, one hand raised in a Tonto goodbye. The shadows behind him were Trina, Libby, and one-eyed Calvin. One by one they stepped into the glare and squinted, all at once discovered for who they were, creatures of the darkness who could not stand the light.

Silvio watched over his kerchief and I could not tell if he was smiling, but I believe he was.

On my island now I can watch the sun come up over water, gray and misty, and I can watch it also disappear into the bowl of pink shimmering water, and those are the times I like best, the twilight before dawn when you can see whatever you want to out there in the offing, the dusky afterburn of the daylight when the world melts into a soft dream of memory.

I dreamed last night of Kanatauk Ridge, the ragged picket line of conifers spiking up on either side, a file of ponies crossing the bare ridge, heads down, their riders silhouetted against a low yellow moon in blotted cameos, a steady procession of them snaking along the saddle of rock, Silvio shadowing Trina, Calvin rocking in the cooling breeze, Libby's short hair riffling gently, Natalia in the lead and Rakes riding trail, keeping them safe for one more night ride, all of them completely anonymous, as happy at that moment as they ever would be in this life.

Gloriana

There are rules about ghosts, as everybody knows. You would not have it any other way.

For instance: ghosts are supposed to be tied to a certain place—a graveyard, say. A ship. A hanging tree along a winding country lane. Especially and most often, a house. A ghost doesn't go wandering all over the neighborhood, stopping here and loitering there, and yet that is exactly what this one did. But then she was a child, and children behave according to the music in their heads, not the logic of grown-up stories.

Another rule is this: in a ghost story, the main character is not supposed to go seeking out the ghost, enticing her to appear, to linger and carve her shape into the air, to move in and take up residence and generally disturb the metaphysical order of things.

And yet that is exactly what Margaret Warren did. She set out deliberately to attract the ghost with toys and candy, the way her neighbors set out hanging jars of red sugar-water to attract hummingbirds.

And let us get this straight at the outset and no mistake: Mrs. Warren's husband, Jack, was a good man but limited by the things he had endured, as such men are. They were passing forty, the two of them, alone in the kind of opulent new house neither one had ever dreamed of affording, she more alone than he, since he was away on business so much. They had married young, and she had given up a position as a retail buyer years ago to help Jack establish a small investment-consulting firm for which she managed the books, from home, figuring the numbers, accounting for things. But the business had grown too successful, too many others working under Jack, and now he had an office suite in the city. Now Margaret no longer kept the books. Now she kept the house, supervised the gardener and the pool man, went on seasonal shopping binges in New York.

Imagine him home at the end of a long week of meetings and consultations, a commuter flight down from the city, with a highball in his hand, thinking about golf and leafing absently through his accumulated mail, and saying how he must leave in the morning for the West Coast and don't worry he'll call right away, and this year St. Maarten seems to be a good bet for December, let's not stay around for Christmas and have to visit the neighborhood round-robin house party and hear them talk about their kids away at Duke and Vassar and Princeton. Always their damned kids.

And Margaret saying with a kind of excitement, "Her name is Gloriana."

"How can you possibly know that?" he says, and the mail is suddenly strewn on the maple sideboard like a deck of oversized playing cards. "Is it somewhere in the records or something?" She has had this strange hobby for weeks, ever since cocktails at the Rupert Markles' when Betty Markle let it slip about the way their toys were littered over the lawn some Saturday mornings, though their own kids were away at camp that summer. Baseballs, frisbees, dolls, and once even a bicycle.

"She told me. Gloriana." Margaret listened to the name pass out of her own mouth like a hymn, an ejaculated prayer, a vote for miracles. She was Catholic and prayed the rosary every Friday since—well, you cannot measure out the meter of eternity.

"So what are you telling me?" In his words the echo of another conversation, two days ago, a therapist friend in the city who said over his third Scotch and soda, "We're all post-Freudians, Jack—you think all you have to do is reach down and yank the trauma out by the roots, like a bad tooth, like extracting the pit of a prune, and voilà—mental health? I'm here to tell you, there are more things in heaven and earth."

"I'm not telling you, Jack. I'm just saying. You listen, then you tell me."

But Jack is tired and doesn't know what he is listening for, not this late. They've been over and over this, and it makes him sad, and he doesn't know what to do about it. And that makes him sadder and a little angry.

Another rule is that a ghost is supposed to remain behind in a sort of limbo with an attitude, assigned by the entity that assigns such things to right some personal wrong that has gone unpunished and unrectified. Usually the act that caused her to die before her time. As everyone knows, ghosts are creatures of justice. They bring order back into the world.

An old widow is poisoned for her gold by a greedy nephew and buried in the basement, and she haunts the premises for three generations until the nephew's grandson learns the bitter truth and gives away his tainted inheritance to charity, and the haunting is lifted.

That's how it works. You presume the ghost knows her mission.

But Gloriana was a happy ghost. In life she had been a housemaid, Negro or sharecropper white, a girl of nine or ten or twelve, depending on who told the story. When Betty Markle told it, after half a bottle of Chablis, her eyes shone with a kind of nostalgia, a mild longing:

Gloriana, she said—Gloriana only came out to play.

She did not do housework, not after death. Instead she swung on porch gliders, borrowed dolls and undressed them, rearranged the furniture in Barbie's Dreamhouse, and invited the stuffed animals to tea. She loved balls—soccer balls and kickballs and tennis balls. And skates, the kind with rubber wheels the best. She loved party dresses and balloons, the colored lights that sprouted every

Christmas, draped across hedges and candy-striped around lampposts, loved to unscrew the bulbs from their sockets and walk around with them still glowing in her hands. And she loved sugary desserts drenched in meringue and chocolate icing. She would take them right out of refrigerators and hide the empty plates outside under the chaise longue.

Betty Markle was a private tennis pro with a good body, supple and brown as a boy's baseball glove, and she gave lessons on a private court two doors down from the Warrens. She said, "The poor girl died in a fire." Betty Markle waved a cigarette in the air, making wreaths of smoke, but she never put it to her lips. "They say she worked for a woman who didn't trust her not to run away. They say the girl was locked in the pantry when it happened, and the old house burned down around her. This was a century ago. More. Back when such things happened."

Which house, where? Margaret wanted to know—perhaps it had stood on the lot she and Jack now owned—but no one knew, exactly. That was back in the days when the old watermen and their families lived in shacks along the Turtle Haul, which was just a sandy lane then, not yet gentrified, the ruts shoveled in with oyster shells that crackled under the steel tires of their wagons, and led down to the water, where they kept broad, shallow-hulled boats for working their crab pots and dredging the oyster beds in the sound.

The turtle captains, aristocracy, kept their deepwater boats moored to stakes in the sound and brought their catch ashore at the landing only at high tide, live barnacle-studded boulders swaddled in seaweed, and they lived in the three or four big frame houses with separate kitchens at the back, because the cooking was all done on open stove fires. It was one of those big houses with all the porches. Gloriana worked for the wife of a turtle captain who was gone to sea for weeks at a time, trailing his lines in the Gulf Stream as he sailed slack against it, sailing in place.

The first time Margaret saw Gloriana, the girl was standing by the back fence, absently flipping a yo-yo in one hand, looking beyond the fence to something Margaret couldn't see. Because of her tatty blue cotton shift and brown bare feet, Margaret recognized her at once. The girl had soft black hair that lifted in the slight breeze and was not contained by the white hair band. Margaret said softly, "Sweetheart, didn't it hurt?"

"It hurt bad, but then it was over."

"How can you be happy?" Margaret said.

The girl shrugged and never turned. "It don't hurt now."

"What are you doing here anyway?" Margaret found herself becoming agitated. She wanted some help with this, some sense, some signal of what was to come next.

"Gloriana just playing." There is a kind of singsong child's voice that mocks adult seriousness on purpose.

"But listen: what are you doing here?" Margaret insisted.

Gloriana didn't understand the question. "If you want me to, I'll go."

Margaret thought it was a kind of test. "No," she said quickly, "don't go. Stay."

"Gloriana can go. She can."

"No—"

But Gloriana was already gone. Margaret could hear the breeze of her passing rattle the stiff leaves of the live-oak. It was a gray day that got inside you and made you feel as if something, somewhere, were terribly wrong, so she deliberately made herself imagine desert skies, cactus, a blazing sun that was always directly overhead so that a person's shadow pooled at her feet like a discarded towel.

And then she went into the house alone and cried.

Because this is what I know that she doesn't know I know: Margaret recognized the child's voice.

A ghost can learn voices. It is a commonplace that ghosts are frozen in time, that when they die they remain exactly the same age they were in life, with exactly the same appearance, thinned a little because of the way light is strained through the ghostly vapors, but otherwise unchanged. And yet nothing could be further from the truth. Ghosts are caught in the act of becoming. They have something to learn, or they wouldn't still be hanging around. And they must learn a way of telling what they know, and to do this they must fool, dissemble, trick, masquerade, and lie.

Because a ghost is a memory of truth, a dream walking, truer than facts.

So when Margaret cried, she was crying over something bigger than the ghost of a long-dead serving girl twirling her homemade yo-yo, glimpsed in the garden looking beyond a fence.

"Let me tell you a story," Betty Markle said that same night while the men were in the garage checking out her husband's new sports car after the Warrens had gone home. "Don't ask me how I know this, I just know it." And she glanced at them all one by one to make sure they were listening. She herself was a bit exuberant from the wine, seeing the room as a wavy splurge of color and the women as her truest friends. "It happened in Mexico. It was in a little village with filthy whitewashed walls and dirty kids running the streets and a sun that beat your brains in."

It was an old story: a boy has wandered far from his life. He gets into trouble here, then there. He steals a car in the middle of the night and smacks it into a light pole, and where did he get the beer anyhow? Somebody's been stealing cash from Jack Warren's top bureau drawer and if there's one thing he can't abide it's a thief, especially one who lies about it. There's the bad crowd, the sullen pale boys who drop out of high school and keep hanging around, smoking and wearing black leather and hard looks, and he runs with them and gets nabbed breaking and entering and there's even a possible statutory rape charge, and Jack does his best work as a father and talks and pays and makes some promises and does not beat the hell out of his son, though someone else does late one night (always late at night), over some screwed up deal involving drugs or money or both, and his mother fetches him home from the emergency room where his nose was repaired and his broken arm set in plaster, and he doesn't say word one.

The gunshot through the living room window, right in the middle of the evening news, that is the last straw. This is before they lived on the Turtle Haul. "Your wild friends don't belong in this place," Jack Warren says, and Margaret agrees, tearfully, but pleading another chance for her little boy.

But he's not a little boy. He's a heroin addict, the doc at the ER said this, and Jack says, "Your drugs don't belong in my house. They go, or you."

So the boy goes. Twice he calls, from Texas, from California, incoherent, sobbing: send money. Each time Jack stands firm until the hours of Margaret's ragged crying have worn him down, and he decides from now on, wherever the damned boy is, whatever he wants, just give it to him. Just so he doesn't come home. This is the boy who wanted to be a priest. When he was a little boy, this is. Not since—but you can't measure out time like that.

Then he calls again, middle of the night, the kid only comes out at night. Mexico. Someplace deep down below the border, lost in Chihuahua between the iguanas and the mescaline whores. Same old story and Jack is reaching for his credit card to tell Western Union when Margaret says, "Tell him to come home."

"We don't want him home," Jack says, holding his palm over the receiver, afraid of losing the tenuous connection. "He won't come anyway."

"Tell him. No more. No more money. No more anything. Unless he comes home." That's it. What was she thinking? I can't tell you, Betty Markle admits. But it's different being a mother, that's all. Just different. The ache is different, the longing more dangerous, it makes you first softer and then harder.

Betty Markle's version: there must have been other calls to break a mother's heart, calls that Jack never knew about. To harden her heart toward her son. To let him slip away. But good luck trying to have it all make sense, Betty Markle says. Just another ghost story, and that's all the logic there is.

The boy's name was Woodrow. That was the name on the luggage tag when they shipped his body home. Slashed his wrists in a hotel room, lay in blood and flies for two days before anybody found him. No note. Scrawled across the bathroom mirror in some girl's lipstick: *wish you were here . . .*

Now Margaret spends her days looking for Gloriana, enticing her to appear. She has rummaged through the garage and found some of Woodrow's old toys, a wagon, a basketball, a tennis racquet. She has set up the Fourth of July barbecue croquet set permanently on the back lawn and left the mallets and balls in the rack near the back steps.

The neighbors notice and talk, and some of them resent the way she has lured their neighborhood ghost away from their backyards, and some of them are just embarrassed for her.

And Gloriana does appear, but always out of the corner of Margaret's eye, never face-on, often invisibly in the night—leaving evidence of scattered croquet balls and overturned wagons on the lawn. For Margaret, it is agonizing consolation. She wonders how long before Jack will leave her. She knows she is giving him no choice.

And one night, many weeks later, she dreams. It is a vivid dream, as if she is watching a late movie with a fluttering picture. A bedraggled girl locked in a small room. Canned goods lining the shelves with labels printed by hand with a laundry marker. A barrel of flour. A sack of sugar. A candle. A match. The girl is smiling like sin and striking the match and lights the candle, and with the candle flame she lights the bundled straw broom, and the walls glow in the sudden flare of light. And the screen goes yellow and then white, and the girl's smile is gone, and then she is outside watching the big house burn a hole in the night.

When Margaret wakes, startled, the teasing voice is hanging in the air: "Gloriana did it." A live voice, out of the dream.

Gloriana burned the house down.

No one else was home.

The turtle captain was far at sea, never to return, for that very night a storm took his boat with all hands. His wife, who would not hear of her husband's disaster for a week, was visiting a man who made nets. Her own children were already dead from yellow fever two years, and the night lonelies had gotten her. Gloriana turns the house into a ghost story, and the captain is left out forever and the children, too. The only other one to keep Gloriana company in the story is the woman who did not trust her to not run away. That's how it is. A mother's grief weighs on Gloriana.

And now Margaret Warren lies next to her husband and listens to every second of the night ratchet past. There is no other way to get through it. Time clicks along, second by second, the gears of the universe turning her slowly toward her new life, tooth by steel tooth, very slowly, so that it will take a long time, so much time there is no guarantee she will see it through to the new life on the other side. She cannot do this alone, and Jack is sunken in his own grief, the deep hard grief of a man who blames only himself for the evil of the world, who cannot understand how he could lose such control over events, over his only son, a husband who knows his wife wants him to leave her, a man who has never been to Mexico and does not plan to go.

It is an irreparably beautiful night, a night of shattered stars strewn across an India ink sky, when restive spirits walk the fields and the peaceful churchyard dead rise with the sickle moon and sigh among the tombstones, their smoky breath lifting toward the black splayed branches of the live-oaks, drifting in a silver band of lucent memory along the Turtle Haul, over the dewy lawn to the single carriage lamp beside the front door of Margaret Warren's house.

Where I am to work now and once more earn my keep.

Stepping Into Flight

It was Brigit's idea. On the third day of our honeymoon, we stood on the crest of Jockey's Ridge, at Kitty Hawk, looking down on our landing zone, which seemed impossibly far away.

"What if we crash?" I'd asked her, trudging up the dune. "What if I can't do it?"

"Take a chance," she had said. "Live a little."

Half a mile from here—after three crash landings—the Wright brothers had piloted the first powered airplane onto the sea breeze. We were about to launch nylon-and-aluminum hang-gliders onto that same wind. We were high enough to see the ocean, rough and wind-chopped.

Among us was another young couple, Chad and Rena. They'd been married for four years, but, due to demanding careers, they had not taken a vacation together in all that time. This was their chance to relax and get to know one another again. They'd told us all this while we watched a training video at the kite shop and signed releases against lawsuits in case we were maimed or killed in flight. Chad was tan and fit from racquetball lunch-hours. He had those aging boyish features common to successful American men in their middle years.

Rena was plain and quiet and wore her brown hair short. She looked like somebody who lived in Connecticut. Trouble was, Rena was petrified of hang-gliding.

The breeze was brisk but fickle, veering and shifting. "Need a volunteer," the head instructor said. "To test the wind."

Brigit raised her hand.

"Show them how easy it is," the instructor said. He strapped her into the harness and she launched herself into the sky—well, not quite. Just about the instant she got enough lift to fly, the wind quit and she nosed hard into the sandy slope.

Since the pilot of a hang-glider "hangs" under the wing, she took the brunt of the crash with her body. She shook the sand out of her clothes and trudged gamely up the dune.

Rena bit her lip and stared at Brigit, as if she envied her.

DURING THE FIRST WEEK of our honeymoon, the other cottages around us were vacant. It was still weeks before the start of the real season, so we were getting a break on the rate. We'd sit on one of the high decks in the afternoon, sipping one of fourteen bottles of champagne we'd brought along, and read out loud to one another from the guest journal.

"Couple from Ohio," I read to her. "'The island is much farther from home than we calculated. We arrived late and now must leave earlier than planned. God must have plans for us on the road home.'"

"Let me see that." Brigit took the journal, flipped some pages, and read another entry. "Surfers from Florida," she said. "Listen: 'Legend of 8-foot tubular monsters lured us from Canaveral. Day One: flat, bummer. Day Two: flat and glassy, bummer—'"

"Skip ahead."

"'Day Nine: hurricane warning—awesome sets!'"

Another day, we sat indoors watching a gentle rain. The sky was purple, and the rain was bright as silver coins.

I came across an entry written by a woman who organized group fasts.

"For a living?" Brigit asked. "How can you organize a fast?"

"She brought a gang of her followers to this house—"

"Followers? People actually have followers?"

"The idea was to 'purge their bodies and purify their spirits, to take away fear and discontent. To even them out.'" Day One's entry was a long explanation of her method—at first, to eat nothing and drink only water. After three days, you were allowed to eat one kind of fruit.

"For how long?" Brigit asked.

"For another three days. If you're still alive after six days, you may eat a second variety of fruit."

Brigit shook her head and scooped up a handful of water crackers and brie, then topped off her glass from the Taittinger's.

I kept reading: "'Day Two: What a perfect place for a group fast! A charming cottage for warm human encounters. The many large bedrooms on two floors make for privacy, yet the great room provides a meeting space big enough for us all. The many decks, especially the one on the roof, allow us ample fresh air and sun. The beach is just over the dunes, and we will make an excursion there every morning and evening.'"

"Sounds like a real-estate brochure," Brigit said.

The fasting woman's handwriting was brisk and neat, full of curlicues and exclamation points.

"'Day Three: Why isn't there more lounge furniture in this house? When one is fasting, it is strenuous to have to sit upright all the time.'" The handwriting looked a little hurried, with a minimum of curlicues—as if she were conserving her strength.

"Sounds like things are unraveling a bit."

By Day Four, her tone had taken on a decided edge: "'Joni and Marie are sulking. Debbie is bored. Jack won't leave his upstairs room. Too weak to climb stairs and check on him.'"

"My God—you think he's still up there?" Brigit laughed.

Day Five's handwriting was ragged and sloppy: "'Jack downstairs now, sleeps on couch. Nobody goes up to roof anymore. Why isn't there more lounge furniture?'"

By Day Six, the handwriting had deteriorated to an almost illegible scrawl. Brigit and I could make out only one part of the entry. We read it out loud together: "'Why was house built so far from ocean? Would like to go to beach, but too far. No one has strength. We look out window, longing . . .'"

The final notation was in someone else's handwriting—that the group had departed, leaving behind a mess of fruit rinds and banana peels.

On Jockey's Ridge, the instructor said, "We'll try going off in the other direction." The wind proved steadier on the other slope, toward the ocean.

We took turns buckling into harness, lifting the kite by the struts, grasping the steering bar, taking a few big strides, then stepping—just plain *stepping*—into the air. It's a miraculous feeling. Your stomach lifts off first. You look down and see your feet still moving, but now they're kicking air. You soar, going fast, trying to play the wind. Then the ground comes up way too quickly, and you get a mouthful of sand.

After that first flight, Brigit was a natural, making long, controlled glides and landing on her feet. I swooped and stalled erratically, landing on my belly and plowing up sand at the end of each flight. But I loved the flying—the transcendent feeling of weightlessness. I was surprised—I hate losing control. But stepping into the air, somehow it thrilled me. I couldn't get enough of it.

Meanwhile, Rena would not go off the ridge. She'd buckle on the harness, take a few deep breaths to get up the nerve, then shake her head. Chad tried to coax her on. "This is costing us a lot of money," he reminded her. She apologized.

She didn't cry—though I could tell she wanted to. Once, she even lifted the kite and began her takeoff, but then she stopped short at the edge of the dune. She could not take the leap. The instructor said, "No big deal. Do it some other time."

Chad said, "Come on, honey—give it one more try."

She gave him a look and then stared off into the distance, beyond Highway 12 to the ocean, breathing deeply, deliberately, biting her lip bloody. Standing there, not stepping.

FOR A WHOLE WEEK, we'd hit the beach in the morning and spend the afternoons sipping champagne on the high decks, watching the gulls wheel and the ocean flex and shimmer. Enjoying the solitude and quiet.

At the start of our second week, neighbors arrived.

First a pickup truck pulled into the driveway next door. An elderly couple got out. Half an hour later, a young couple arrived in a van. The woman carried a squawling infant. The man slid back the cargo door and out tumbled four kids, like dice spilling out of a cup.

All afternoon, vehicles kept arriving. Clearly some kind of family reunion was in progress. Every woman seemed to have at least one infant. One of the mothers looked no more than fifteen years old. So many people were coming and going that, after we had counted twenty people, we lost track.

The last vehicle to arrive was a bored-out Firebird towing a glittering boat. Off its stern hung two of the biggest outboard engines I'd ever seen.

Our new neighbors raised a ruckus all night long. We didn't especially mind the music or the laughter, but the shouting and arguing began to wear on us.

Next day at the crack of dawn one of the young men hauled out a long fishing pole thick as a rifle barrel, dangling hooks big enough to anchor a small boat. Accompanied by five of the others, he left with the boat.

Every morning they'd go out fishing. Every afternoon, when they returned, I'd call over, "Catch anything?" The only replies I ever got were sullen stares.

One afternoon on a whim, Brigit and I went out on a party boat for two hours and came back with a mess of Spanish mackerel.

I cleaned them on the table under the cottage. Our neighbor fishermen stood under their carport and glowered at me.

Next day, a gale blew in—thirty knot winds. The cottage shuddered and creaked on its pilings. Our neighbors decided to launch a kite off their back deck. Almost immediately it became entangled with the only power line for three hundred yards around. For the rest of the week it hung there—a black, bat-shaped kite flapping like a wounded bird. The kind of sound that keeps you up at night.

They ran the air conditioner constantly, yet their windows were always open. Their babies were always crying, and nobody ever seemed to pay attention. Heavy metal screamed from a boom box on their deck. They shouted and cursed and fought, swarming over the cottage, their fleet of vehicles roaring up and down our little cul-de-sac at all hours of the day and night.

"They have no idea where they are, what's going on around them," Brigit said one night. "This whole place, it's lost on them."

Brigit stood in the doorway, hip cocked, back to me, the breeze riffling her blonde hair, and I thought, "Not me—I know exactly where I am," and watched her until she turned, and felt as if she'd stood in the doorway of my house all our lives. It shouldn't have been a romantic moment, but it was.

One of the last afternoons of our honeymoon, Brigit and I were sitting together looking at photographs when we heard three sharp pops. "Get down!" I said. "That's rifle fire." We heard another burst of sharp reports, then quiet. After a few minutes, I cautiously opened our door and peered out.

Across the lot from me, standing on his deck, .22 rifle cradled in the crook of his arm, stood one of our neighbors. "Good thing I brought along my snake gun," he said, beaming. An older man patted him on the back. He pointed under our cottage, where a dead snake lay blasted shapeless. "Cottonmouth," he said.

Brigit held my hand. "Did we bring along any guns?"

"No," I said. "Don't worry."

"Too bad. How about the *Veuve Clicquot* this afternoon?"

AT THE END OF the afternoon on Jockey's Ridge, Chad and Rena walked ahead of us down the dune and across the sandy flat to the highway. He didn't have his arm around her—they walked separately. Rena looked embarrassed beyond words. Chad kept saying, "We can't get a refund, but they said they'll give you a wind-check." Their version of a rain-check.

"I don't want a wind-check," she said. "I just don't want to do this." They walked across Highway 12 and got into their car. We never saw them again.

I can imagine them in the car on the way back to their rental cottage. She says, "What in the world ever led you to think I'd go jumping off cliffs with you?"

He says, "I thought it would be good for you to be daring for a change."

But I don't know whether they said anything at all. Probably they just went back to their lives and never mentioned it again. If he was a nice guy, he gave her flowers once in a while for no reason. But he could never take back what he did to her on that ridge in front of all those strangers—how he'd forced her to make a private choice in public.

That night, a hard rain hammered the island. The wind gusted along the high decks, sliding the wooden chairs into a pile. Brigit and I lay in bed, holding each other, listening to the house creak and shudder. At midnight, we were still awake. The bed was rocking like a boat. The whole house was swaying, as if it were underway, cruising through the storm, lashed by surf and driven by tide. We held on, thrilled. The rain splashed against the window, and for all we knew we were already miles out at sea, adrift.

After the storm passed, we heard the neighbors moving out, loading their caravan like the circus leaving town. In the morning, we saw the mountain of trash they'd left behind: a mound of empty diaper boxes, two trash barrels full of beer cans, a stack of plastic bags full of garbage, half a dozen splintered shafts of wood—who knows where they came from.

And, sticking up out of the barrel of beer cans like a mast, a deep-sea-fishing pole, tangled in nylon filament line and snapped clean in two.

Later that day, the black kite finally blew free of the power line and disappeared over the dunes. Our neighbors were gone. Now they were somebody else's neighbors. We climbed onto our high deck and uncorked our last bottle of champagne.

NOW IT'S MIDWINTER. WE'RE down in the dumps, slogging through our daily routine. As we hunt through a box of tax receipts, we come across the certificates they awarded us that day—the ones that prove we flew off Jockey's Ridge last summer on our honeymoon. The ones Chad and Rena never got, like the Spanish mackerel our honeymoon neighbors never caught.

We smile. Brigit turns to me and says, "Let's go flying again."

I remember what it feels like to step into flight and swoop through thin air, sailing along on pure, unreasonable faith. There are no guarantees. It never evens out. I don't want it to even out, hard landings and all. "Yeah, why not," I say. "Let's go flying again."

"Great," she says. "Next summer. To Paris."

Miracle Boy

Eddie Panek was just another suburban kid until he fell down a well at the age of seven—the age of reason, for us Catholics. In his own backyard, a tract house in Dover, Delaware. The well was a leftover from the days when that country was all farmland, the barnwood cover hidden under sod and finally rotted through. They searched five hours before they found him.

In falling, the boy impaled his right hand on a nail in one of the old boards. A square, hand-forged nail from another century.

When he dove into that hole, he went to sleep and never woke up. So little blond Eddie Panek, who fell through the earth and never quite landed, became the Miracle Boy.

Not right away. First there were the months in the hospital, the wake at his bedside, the procession of believers. I heard all this later, doing a piece for *The Examiner*, up in the city. His fame had spread out, become a rumor at cocktail parties, a phone call from a friend who knew a friend who knew a friend. Eddie had been in a coma for three years. And now people were claiming miracles.

I drove down there on a bright cold morning when the fields of corn stubble lay bent under a crust of old snow, and dirty ice scabbed the shoulder of Highway 13.

The house was typical FHA ranch style, needing paint, and they had turned the garage into a sort of chapel, with a walk-through corridor so the pilgrims could file past Eddie's adjustable hospital bed, out of reach behind plexiglass. The boy lay there still, blond curls tousled on the pillow, a pale-blue blanket drawn up to his chin. The right hand loosely open, the palm healed into a star of white proud flesh.

A ventilator soughed rhythmically up and down, forcing air into his lungs. Red ribbons fluttered off the vent of a heater mounted into the wall behind him. High above the head of his bed hung a small wooden cross. I thought the cross was odd—a Catholic should have had a crucifix. Except for the cross, the wall was white, newly painted, lustrous as a movie screen. This was the wall on which the image was said to appear. On our side of the glass, a rack of votive candles burned, but there was no coin box.

The family allowed visitors only on Fridays and holy days. They waited patiently in single file down the driveway and up the block, huddled in the cold, not talking much. A woman with a blue goiter on her neck explained on my first visit, "They didn't used to have the glass. But some people would tear off swatches of the Miracle Boy's blanket for relics, you see, they shredded it like moths." She worked her fingers like big insects. "And so they had to put up glass. I don't blame them." And she nodded her head once, with finality, her goiter bobbing. She came faithfully every week, in case a miracle happened. Any miracle. I'd seen her kind before, most often gathered at the site of a terrible accident on the highway. Her life was a long pause between moments when terrible, exciting things happened to other people, when she licked at the edges of the drama.

I watched the pilgrims file past the bed, touching their fingertips to the plexiglass, or kissing it, leaving a smudge of breath. Glancing furtively at the wall under the cross, afraid that if they looked directly at it, they would jinx their chance at a vision of the miraculous.

There was an old woman in a wheelchair, three or four others leaning on crutches, canes, and walkers.

There was a blind boy with a white shepherd dog on a harness, and a teenaged girl who looked like she'd been crying all her life.

And there were three little black girls in a row, holding hands, with horribly disfigured faces—sisters, burned when their tree caught on fire on a Christmas morning when they were infants.

Three or four young women held fussing babies, and one clutched the hand of a little boy with Down syndrome so hard I thought she must be hurting him, but he only smiled broadly.

A white-haired man hawked constantly into a blue kerchief— TB, what used to be called *consumption*. The thing that eats you from the inside out.

These people just showed up, sprung loose from some enclave where lived all the damaged, unsightly, faltering people of the region, praying for a cure. I was transfixed by them, felt a strange and thrilling attraction. I stared at them rudely and without apology. I used to believe that suffering brought redemption, but here I saw only suffering.

All these lost souls.

I interviewed them without guile. They talked their lives into my tape recorder and felt honored to do so, as if I were saving them from oblivion. You can walk right up to strangers and they will confide their most intimate secrets, and then they are astonished to discover themselves in the newspaper in a way they do not recognize.

None of the pilgrims looked rich. None of them, except the Down's boy, looked happy. It was hard to say any of them even looked hopeful. But they possessed an unreasoning faith. Perhaps it grew out of their suffering, the will and effort and courage the world required of them at every waking instant. A stubborn intestinal fortitude so necessary, so routine, they took it for granted.

"And what have you come to ask for?" Mrs. Panek said suddenly. Her first name was Helen, but I wouldn't dare call her by her first name. She was a slight woman with a hard, inscrutable face and she appeared all at once, almost violently, behind the storm door. Slavic, I thought. A face from Ellis Island four generations ago. A face that would not be turned back.

"Nothing," I told her. "I'm the reporter."

"I know," she said patiently in a quiet, flinty voice. "That's not what I asked. What do you want from him?" Her tone reminded me of the bishop's at confirmation, twenty-five years ago, just before he slapped me so hard he almost knocked me loose from the altar rail. The slap is meant to be symbolic—you're becoming a soldier for Christ—but our bishop was in a holy rage that evening and he stung me hard with the fact of his righteous anger, at whom or what, I never discovered. But being a Catholic is like that—things fall on your head all at once, and you don't question the violent mystery.

"Nothing," I said. "Not me. My editor sent me down for a piece."

"You will, then," she said. "Sooner or later. All of them want something from him."

THE MIRACLES HAD STARTED in the second year of his coma.

A mother came to beseech Eddie to find her child, lost in the woods for a week, and almost immediately the little girl was discovered safe, asleep under a tree. Mrs. Panek used that word, *beseech*. The woman said she had had a dream of a boy in a hospital bed and learned about Eddie through a neighbor.

Two or three other children recovered lost dogs or cats. A little wheezing boy came to gawk, and suddenly his asthma went away. A pregnant woman who had cancer came by faithfully every week and discovered, upon going into labor, that her cancer had disappeared, and the baby was born healthy.

They were all equivocal miracles—that is, a rational explanation could account for all the cases. But there was a sort of underground of the faithful, and for them the chance for small miracles, equivocal miracles, was enough. More than three hundred people tramped through his bedroom, staring at little Eddie, oblivious in his coma. To save wear and tear on their home, the Paneks built the garage addition.

This is all in my notes.

Then came the Hollywood moment: a five-year-old boy hobbling by in metal leg-braces, his bones all twisted up from some pre-natal infection. There were actual x-rays to show that his bones were deformed and he was crippled in a way no surgeon could change. They say he paused at the glass, his mouth dropped open as if it had been hooked, and he pressed his palms to the glass and fell into a kind of trance, staring at the white wall behind the bed. They say that Miracle Boy's eyes fluttered, perhaps even opened for a split second—and then the lame boy calmly unstrapped his braces and walked away on perfect legs.

I could not document this—the doctor had since passed away and the little boy who was cured had moved to a different city. The x-rays had vanished. That's always the case with miracles—they seem to require distance and a shadowy provenance. Up close, in the glare of scrutiny, they evaporate—explained away as exaggeration, as coincidence, as hope gone awry.

"Where is Mister Panek?" I asked Helen Panek. The door was open and the cold wind was drafting into her house in fitful gusts and she didn't flinch. She invited me in and we sat on her floral couch and she did not offer me coffee and I could have used some.

She said, quietly, "This has been hard on Walter. He works a second shift at the box factory now on some days, to pay for all this." The ventilator, the room addition, the candles, the maintenance, the electricity.

That was my slant, of course, the thing my editor had sent me down to expose: who was gaining what from all this mumbo-jumbo. That it was all just mumbo-jumbo. But I hadn't seen a collection box, a donation plate, tithing envelopes, nothing to show cash was changing hands. Every person I asked said he had not left anything behind but good wishes. The only *gifts* the Miracle Boy received were crutches, leg braces, canes, all of them child-sized, draped with scapular medals, St. Jude medals, rosaries. And cut flowers that withered quickly, and homemade get-well cards, crayon drawings of the Virgin Mary on construction paper. It was a damned poor way to cash in.

"We did not ask for this," Mrs. Panek said that Friday, as we sat behind her lacy living room curtains—the kind of curtains second-generation immigrants always hang because they hint of something finer, a lightening of the dark sky of the Old Country— seeing the shadows of the faithful shuffling up her walk to the garage, specters against the gray afternoon light. "It sickens me, all the pain. What they ask for. The old ones. He can only do little miracles. He's a kid."

"He's ten now?"

"He is seven years old and always will be."

I wondered briefly how old she herself was—by her hands, not more than thirty-five, but her face had a gray cast, deep lines etched around her eyes, sorrow cleaved into her brow. She could be staring out of a sepia photo of the fall of Warsaw.

It made no sense. Why hadn't she left the boy in the care of the hospital? Why didn't she just close her home to strangers? Why did she put up with this? What was she getting out of it?

"You don't believe in miracles," she said.

"You believe in miracles?"

"Of course not," she said. "Not before. Never before. My God." "But now."

Her gaze was direct and steady and felt on me the way a cop's eyes do when he's looking you over to decide if you're sober enough to get back behind the wheel. "There's no way I can say this without sounding crazy, when you write it up," she said, and crossed her hands in her lap, as if resigned to being dismissed as a lunatic, as if she didn't care what I thought of her. As if she were long past that level of things. She lifted a hand, brushed her ash-blonde hair behind her ear. "He spoke to me, he said to take him home. Take him home, and they would come to him."

"At the hospital?"

"I was in the hospital chapel, praying. After Eddie had already been in a coma for months, this is. A man I had never met before was suddenly sitting there beside me. A handsome man with, how can I say this, compassionate eyes. Eyes that looked at you and did not blink. Eyes that made you want to tell what was in your heart." She stared at me until I didn't look away. "I thought he was a young doctor. He laid his hand on my arm and I felt this sort of charge, a sting like electricity. He said, 'Take the boy home and let him do his work.'"

"And since then? It's been three years—"

"It is so hard to lose a child. I think sometimes I can hardly bear it. I think this way may be the hardest of all."

"Do you hear voices?"

She laughed tiredly. "You want me to admit to being a kook. All right, I hear his voice sometimes. Eddie's. He whispers to me sometimes. He'll say, 'That one, Mom. This one, Mom. I'm sorry, I can't, Mom.' Sometimes it's just a feeling as I watch one or another of those who come to ask him for a miracle. I can see a kind of glow if they will be helped." She looked at the tape recorder until I clicked it off. "And of course, they say there is the image."

"You see the image?"

"No. I would never claim that." She crossed herself.

"How often do you see this glow?"

"Less and less now." She sighed. "He is not strong now. In the beginning, he was stronger. Now, they want more and more, bigger and bigger miracles." Her eyes were blinking back tears and she suddenly looked very young.. "But his work is only for children. Only little miracles for the kids."

"Do they leave donations?"

"They try. We can't take them. Walter—my husband—he thinks we should, to pay for all this. But the man in the hospital chapel told me not to." She paused, as if debating whether or not to tell me the rest. "He said: Let no money change hands on account of suffering."

Then she said again, "What do *you* want from him? Why have you come?"

I expected nothing. I told her this.

"You have a family?"

"No more," I said.

"Divorce?"

We were going around a gentle turn at less than twenty-five miles per hour and the sun was in my eyes, just for a second. It was none of her business. "No, not divorce."

"There is nothing he can do."

"I don't want him to do anything." She died from glare. My daughter. A little bump into a fence post. Her head against the dashboard. There wasn't even any blood. It had been nine years. Her face had faded. Let me tell you what suffering is. It isn't a lost dog or a gimpy leg or even a child's asthma. It's that you were a good and careful father, and just once you got blinded by the sun on the windshield when you didn't expect it, just once you couldn't see exactly where you were going, just one second of one minute of one day of your life, and you can't take it back, and you can't reclaim it through penance because the sin was too trivial even to require absolution.

FOR THE NEXT SEVERAL months, I drove fifty miles down from the city and kept track of the miracles. The little ones:

A girl carried in her poisoned puppy, limp and dying, and at the glass bedside it perked up all at once, yelped for joy, and vomited out the poison.

A baby covered with boils was laid before the glass, and the boils healed instantly—like time-lapse photography.

A four-year-old boy had never spoken a word until suddenly, pressed to the glass, he pointed at the white wall and cried "Mama!" and the crowd dropped to their knees and crossed themselves, though no one else saw what the child was seeing on the white wall.

And the big miracles:

The boy who recovered from leukemia.

The blind girl who got back her vision.

The runaway kid with amnesia who wandered onto the property and immediately remembered his name and called home from the Paneks' kitchen.

I kept track of these miracles, though I don't claim I witnessed them. Fourteen Fridays, altogether, I spent at the Paneks', but I was never present for a single miracle. I do not claim either that I doubted them—who am I to make any claim about the truth of what another person believes?

In any case, as the miracles mounted, as I reported them in my newspaper, the crowds grew, as if this were all leading up to something. The diocese sent a monsignor to investigate. He quietly threatened the family with excommunication if they encouraged further heresy. Mrs. Panek let me stay for the interview. Mr. Panek— Walter—sat beside her, silent, wearing starched blue coveralls, his face clean-shaven and pale and angry, and held her hand.

"God does not favor idolaters," the priest said gently.

"I am a good Catholic," Mrs. Panek said. "I have always obeyed the church."

"Then put a stop to this talk of miracles."

"I have no control over it, Father. I have no choice."

"Have you talked to your parish priest about this?"

"I have confessed. I have asked for guidance." Mr. Panek gripped her hand in both of his and nodded. "But the people keep coming. All we have done is try to make it as pleasant as possible for all of us."

"You love these people, then. You love the attention, yes? You love the way they look at you for something wonderful to happen?"

Mrs. Panek looked him in the eye and said, "I loathe these people. They are my penance."

The monsignor spent some minutes writing this all down. Then he said, "Do you claim the intercession of the Blessed Virgin Mary?"

Mrs. Panek said, "I claim nothing."

The monsignor said, "But does she appear to the boy? To you? To either of you?"

Husband and wife glanced at each other and then quickly looked away, but not quickly enough.

"So she has appeared?"

"Not to us."

"Then to whom?"

"There are those who say that—who say that they see her image on the wall behind Eddie's bed. Under the cross. The image of the Blessed Mother leaning over the boy. As if she is nursing him."

"Does the boy see her?"

"It is not for us to say what the boy sees," Walter Panek said.

The monsignor nodded and wrote some more. It was the first of several visits—usually he came alone, but occasionally he brought another old sly priest with him who still wore the traditional cassock, rather than the crisp modern suit the monsignor wore.

Once the old priest asked, "Why do you hang a cross and not a crucifix over the boy's bed?"

Mrs. Panek answered, "Why does the church worship the image of the dying Christ, and not the risen Christ?"

And the old priest nodded and wrote down what she said, as if perhaps he agreed. "Nevertheless," he prodded, "you should hang a crucifix." And so she did.

Another time, the old priest asked, "What of the stigmata?"

"There is no stigmata," Mrs. Panek said. "When he fell, Eddie put a nail through his hand. That's all."

"And it does not bleed?"

"No, it doesn't bleed."

"If he bleeds from the hands and feet, if he suffers the salt wounds of Christ, that is a sign that faith has overcome doubt. A sign that he has taken on the suffering of others, that he has not despaired, that he might help bring them to redemption through our Lord, Jesus Christ."

"He does not bleed."

The priest nodded with regret and wrote everything down with a sharp pencil.

MY FEATURE HAD RUN in three parts but was long done, interest had moved on, yet I continued to be drawn to the Paneks' home. Helen Panek showed me Polaroids of Eddie in all the usual family poses, and I came to feel as if I'd actually once known him as an ordinary little boy who dug forts in the sandbox and caught toads in the high grass and raced his green tricycle up and down the cracked driveway.

I would stand for an hour or two, watching the parade of broken people pass his bed, staring at the wall under the crucifix for a vision I was certain I would never see. Go home, I wanted to tell them all, you are what you are. You are more than your infirmity. This little boy can't change you.

"Why do you keep coming back?" Mrs. Panek asked me, time and again. I had no answer. All I knew in my heart was that something real was happening at her home, or was about to happen, or had already happened. Something actual, bigger than fame or pity or suffering. Something beyond us. Something earned by the bishop's hard slap. A mystery as big and terrible as a comet or a hurricane or the fall of darkness or a sudden glaze of light across the windshield, something that could not be denied.

I wanted to tell her the story of how I came to be this hollow man who watched at her son's bedside: I was blinded on a lovely day in the country. That's how I lost my daughter. Her death was a stupid, gentle accident that held no meaning, none, and only a very special marriage can survive the loss of a child. We were not special. There was nothing to be done. But of course we do not talk to strangers that way. Our loss does not soften their loss. She had a right to her long, slow grief. As I had a right to mine.

Still, as winter became rainy spring and spring dried up into summer, I visited the Miracle Boy. Knowing he was there, I could not look away.

IN THE END, THE diocese claimed the Miracle Boy. The bishop would celebrate a special Mass on August 15, the Feast of the Assumption of the Virgin Mary body and soul into heaven—to pray for his soul and the souls of all children injured or sick or killed.

At first, the Mass was scheduled for the local parish church, but it soon became obvious that many thousands planned to attend. The church reserved the local college football stadium. The Miracle Boy would be placed in an air-conditioned glass booth at the foot of the altar, to emphasize his low place in the divine scheme of things.

We sat on folding chairs—the parents, their parish priest, me. The bishop celebrated the Mass on a stage erected in the home end zone. The monsignor and the old sly priest served as acolytes. The cathedral choir was bused in from the city, along with schoolchildren from Catholic parishes around the state. It's a small state, and it was no trick to get there.

It was medieval, a look down the barrel of the twelfth century. The bishop and his acolytes in fine golden robes offered a high Mass that stirred the soul with spectacle and the power of chant, and you could feel their voices in your chest, choking your own voice, and it almost brought solace.

At the Offertory, each school group, every delegation of the Knights of Columbus, each chapter of the Altar Society, brought forth a donation to further the church's work with children. They carried to the altar baskets full of fat envelopes of money, and they had no business.

The sky was white, a scorching haze of breathless space. Several women fainted. I sweated through the stiff collar of my white shirt. Helen Panek dabbed at her brow with a handkerchief, steadying herself by gripping the chair back in front of her, and Walter Panek fanned her with a prayer pamphlet.

The heat hammered at my head and made the air swirl and shimmer.

At Communion, the faithful trooped by the Miracle Boy's glass booth and crossed themselves and plodded into the end zone to receive the body and blood of Christ. Mrs. Panek's body went rigid at the sight of the parade of the halt, the lame, the blind, the disfigured, the ruined, the broken, the feeble-minded, the cancerous, the grieving, the children who would never grow up. They were shimmering ghosts, wavy in the heat, unsightly mirages, unspeakably beautiful in their suffering, one by one opening their hands to receive the bread and then grasping the common cup to sip the wine that was the blood of Christ.

Helen Panek knelt while the rest sat, eyes shut, hands pressed hard together in prayer.

I did not take Communion. I was not worthy. It was true—I did want something from the boy. The fact settled on my conscience like a steady warm rain. I wanted to see through the glare. Once and for all. To witness an unequivocal miracle. To be given back not just hope, but my faith, in a blazing instant, as it had been taken from me.

It made me ashamed.

The air was white, as if the mantle of atmosphere had evaporated, leaving only the vacuum of outer space between us and the sun. My palms sweated and itched. I squinted my eyes. The sun grew larger and brighter and suffused the sky with a painful, burning light.

At the finale of the mass, the "Magnificat" rose in majestic tones, a Latin hymn of praise to the Virgin Mother of Christ, and in the white light I saw the still blond boy in the glass booth and watched his parents forever on the other side of the glass. Behind the glass, spangled in shafts of sun glare, I could see the accordion sleeve of the ventilator rise and fall, and the frail body spasm, and the eyes flutter, and the body still, and the ventilator keep rising and falling, and the Mass go on and nobody notice, and there was a sort of glow upon the blue blanket and the blond curls, a kind of rising wavering heat, that fluted like smoke out the top of the glass booth and into the white summer sky, and, outlined in the hot spales of fractured light, a woman's figure was kneeling over the boy.

She was just a shadow moving behind the glass glare, a figure without clean definition, made luminous at the edges by the glare. I squinted against the glare, strained my eyes, but could bring the picture into no clearer focus.

For a second I thought Helen Panek had taken her place inside the booth—but then she tumbled heavily to the grass beside her folding chair, and in fainting she smiled as if hearing the voice of a young doctor telling her everything was going to be all right, and when I looked again, a cloud had erased the image of the woman inside the glass booth into shadow.

I felt a hot stone at the back of my throat, and when I raised the palm of my hand to my mouth, I tasted salt.

Ace

We discovered the airplane the summer after the polio had swept through town and left Skeeter Fitch with his paralyzed left leg strapped into a steel brace. On that June morning, Moe—who was called that because his mother cut his black hair in a bowl-cut like Moe Howard, one of the Three Stooges—led us down the dirt road behind our neighborhood, thick woods on one side and barbed wire fence on the other.

Moe carried a whacking stick, which was just what it sounds like: a long heavy stick he used to whack against trees, fence posts, and other kids who got in his way.

His sidekick, Skeeter, gimped along behind. Skeeter was pale and already filthy, as usual, from rolling on the ground to get away from Moe's whacking stick. Behind him walked Barry Raines—we called him Brains because he was already taking algebra in some sort of brainiac class at Central High School, even though he was only in eighth grade, like the rest of us.

Except my little brother Robbie the Runt. Robbie the Runt was a puny little puke of a kid, my parents' darling, who always got to tag along even though he was three years younger than me. Robbie wasn't a bad kid—didn't say much, did what he was told, never complained. He was just *there*—permanently, eternally *there*. Wherever I went, I would turn around and bump into the kid, and he would give me his goofy grin and just stand there, getting in my way. Robbie the Runt was a smart kid, always reading biographies of George Washington and President Eisenhower and the Wright brothers and about how the Constitution was made. But try to show him how to patch a bicycle tire, and he'd look at you like you just landed from Mars.

At the supper table, our dad would always get Robbie to show off what he was reading. Then he would shoot his cuffs—he always wore his office clothes to the supper table—and say to me, "And what are *you* reading, Marshall?" And he would look at me without blinking through his horn-rimmed glasses and steeple his clean fingers, and I would feel about two inches tall. I didn't read books. Books were hard for me. The letters danced out of reach, and the sentences didn't make a lot of sense unless I went really slow, and then I got bored and started to look out the window or whatever.

But give me a tool, something with weight that you could hold in your hand, a mechanical connection, something that bolted on or screwed in or turned a crank, and I could get lost for hours. I'd rebuilt our lawn mower twice and even tuned the engine in the Buick when Dad was out of town on business, and he never noticed.

I had built a whole squadron of airplane models that hung on wires in the bedroom I shared with Robbie the Runt—not the easy plastic models, but wooden models that came as blueprints and sheets of balsa wood and linen, and you had to cut the struts and frames and stretch the linen over the wings and fuselage and dope it to make it tight, attach little wires to the ailerons so they moved up and down and to the tail rudder so it cocked left or right. I bought them at the Western Auto with money I saved from my paper route. Mr. Rutledge, the manager, would order them for me special.

At night, lying in bed and listening to my parents argue downstairs, I'd stare up at the airplanes and watch them spin slowly in the breeze sifting in from the open window. The streetlight cast their shadows against the far wall, and I'd imagine flying—soaring and diving and looping all over the sky, my fist curled around the joystick, the wind flying past my face, my brother and all his stupid books far below in a miniature world that didn't matter. I'd fall asleep watching their shadows dance across the wall. It was beautiful to see and lifted my heart on bad nights when I lay awake fearing that I would never amount to anything, which was a lot of nights. I miss them even now.

So at the supper table, I would just grin stupidly and say to my dad, "Well, the new Archie comic book is a real hoot." And get sent to my room—again—where I could work on my Sopwith Camel or Gypsy Moth.

Beyond the barbed wire fence lay Old Man Saylor's farm. He never raised anything but a few milk cows and horses, who had the run of the pastures and the creek. The pastures were all overgrown with burrs and blackberry bushes, and wherever an oak tree grew, the space around it was an island of high, dense bramble thicket, ideal for a fort. Our fort in the woods had been bulldozed over during the winter to make room for more cheapo houses in a new subdivision. Now all the woods was surveyed and marked off with stakes, and by the end of the summer, it would all be gone. So we were roaming farther afield, daring for the first time to venture across the barbed wire into unknown territory.

You could see out across the pasture to the creek, the sun already high enough to make us squint. Beyond the creek lay more pastures, more fences. On the rusty barbed wire hung a sign hand-painted in red letters on gray barnwood:

Trespassers wil be persecuted to the fool extend of the LAW
by 2 mongrel DOGS and a 12-gage SHOTGUN
what hain't loded with sofer cushins.

"That don't mean nothing," Moe said. "Them dogs been dead for fifty years." Moe was a raw-boned kid with a head that was too big, his mop of black hair always flopping in his face so that he was constantly slicking it back with his left hand. He'd already done a stint in juvy for breaking into houses, and it was a sure bet he was going back someday soon. His father was a drinker and used to disappear for days on end and sometimes come home in a police car, and none of the grown-ups ever talked about it. Except that Moe was one of the boys we were not allowed to play with.

But Old Man Saylor had a reputation for being eccentric and mean, and just maybe he had *new* mongrel dogs. Maybe he replaced the old mongrel dogs every couple of years, like some people replaced their old cars. Once when I was coming back from fishing the creek farther up the dirt road, I had caught a glimpse of one big, yellow dog loping along the pasture near the house, and of Old Man Saylor himself standing on the porch calling his yellow dog home. He was a tall, bony man dressed all in dungarees, with thick white hair and beard, like an Old-Testament prophet. In those days the only men in our neighborhood who wore beards were the hobos who wandered in from the B&O railroad tracks. Old Man Saylor looked my way and shaded his eyes with a hand, like he was scouting, and I ran all the way home.

Skeeter unlaced the leather straps from his leg brace, stripped it off from his dungarees, and stuffed it behind a bush, the way he always did, so he wouldn't get it all muddy and filthy—or else his old man would whip him with his army belt—then slipped between two strands of wire.

Careful to avoid the cow flop, we humped through the brown grass, already greening up, smelling the humid June air already buzzing with flies and sweet with honeysuckle, scratched our way through brambles, and crossed the creek on stepping stones into the pasture farthest from Old Man Saylor's house. Beyond this field there was one last fence and a long drop into an abandoned borrow pit, a big sandy-clay hole in the earth where dump trucks used to haul out gravel and sand when they built our subdivision. But they didn't go there anymore, not in a long time.

The wind suddenly kicked up out of nowhere—sluicing through a kind of natural funnel between two forested hills over the borrow pit and right into our faces. The grass rustled and hissed, and suddenly the whole pasture seemed to be alive and cooler. The wind lifted my black-and-orange Orioles cap right off my head, and I had to chase it down as it cartwheeled through the high grass.

We crawled on hands and knees through a thicket island into the middle of an open space and inside the shady cave made by a rotten pasture oak and all the brambles. When we stood up and brushed the grass and leaves off our dungarees and t-shirts, we were staring at a dilapidated barn roofed in rusty tin. There it stood, totally invisible from outside the thicket. We pushed through the double front door and saw it had through-and-through double doors, so you could drive equipment in and out without backing up. The back double doors were closed and locked by a heavy wooden bar.

And smack in the center of the dirt floor stood an old airplane—or what was left of one. A glider without an engine, a big box kite really, the wings faded yellow fabric over wooden frames, the ghost of a bright idea, lying there in a shed overgrown with sumac and nettles.

"Too cool!" said Moe, and we swarmed over the glider. On the lower wing was a cradle for a pilot to lie in while flying it. "Out of the cool blue Western sky comes Sky King!" Moe yelled and sprawled onto it and the struts in the wing crunched under his weight.

Brains said, "Get off—you're too heavy! Jeez, what a fat load."

Moe got to his feet. His eyes shone with that look a boy's eyes get when his little brain is hatching a dangerous and stupid idea. He turned to Skeeter. "You thinking what I'm thinking?"

Skeeter grinned. He was always missing teeth. He began flapping his arms. "Wild blue yonder, man," he said.

The glider was in bad shape, the canvas wings moldy, torn in patches. A couple of struts were warped, and some of the braces were cracked. But the shape of the thing was there, a beautifully efficient machine for soaring through the air. I recognized it. I had one just like it hanging from the ceiling of my room: a 1912 Sparrowhawk glider. Two wings, a thin blade of a frame reaching back to a tail section with swallowtail winglets and a curved vertical stabilizer. The little history card that had come with the model kit claimed that the Sparrowhawk had once held the world glider record, soaring for more than an hour off some mountain peak out West. The curved skids on its undercarriage were propped on a kind of wheeled bogie on narrow rusty tracks that disappeared at the back door of the shed—what we now saw was really a hangar.

We had all heard tales of Old Man Saylor, how he had made his fortune inventing gadgets for the army, how he used to fly a private plane right off his pasture. How his only son, Cal Junior, was killed in the Big War, and the old man never went off the place again but holed up in the house with his dogs. He built a cabin on the property for his son's pregnant wife, who died in childbirth, and one night he burned down the cabin on purpose. His twenty-year-old granddaughter Penny had just got married last year. It was in the paper. They had the wedding right on the farm, and none of us knew anybody who was invited.

But I had never heard about any gliders.

The rusty track, like a miniature railroad, ran to the back doors. On an instinct, I removed the wooden bolt from the back doors and flung one of them open. The breeze rushed in and quivered the wings of the glider. From the open door, I could look down the sloping swale of pasture to a small rise, then a dip to the fence, the point where it dropped off into the borrow pit, and a few hundred yards beyond the pit, I could see green grass. I said "Looks like he launched it from right back here, into the wind."

We kicked around in the high grass and discovered the rest of the overgrown steel track that ran down the slope. I walked slowly down the slope and stood at the barbed-wire fence, where a double gate had been fixed at the end of the track and locked by a rusty chain and padlock, looking out across the borrow pit to the other side. The pit had been carved right out of the pasture, and it lay before me like an open wound—sides scraped and scarred, a hundred feet below, the red clay glistening with pools of stagnant, oily water, looking like everything that was missing from my life. The wind was steady on my face. That was why he had launched it from here: the wind. You need wind to generate airspeed over the wings and lift the glider.

The rails ran for maybe a hundred feet to the edge of the pit, about as far as I could throw a baseball.

Moe ran to the fence, jumping up and down with glee, Skeeter and Robbie the Runt close behind. "Jesus H. Christ!" he shouted. "This is going to be the best!"

"That crate ain't in no shape to fly," I reminded him. "It's all rotten."

Moe grabbed me by the collar of my polo shirt. "Don't you want to do something great? I mean something really great? That they'd remember forever and tell stories about? Man, oh man! Jesus H. Christ, Marsh, it doesn't get any cooler than this!"

I said, "It's all busted up."

Moe stood toe to toe with me, so close I could smell him, sour and rank. "You're scared. That's what it is."

"I ain't scared."

"Look at us, Marsh. Take a good look." He spun slowly around, flapping his arms at the woods, the pasture, the sky. "Where are we going? You think I'm going anywhere?"

"High school," I said.

Moe snorted. "Yeah, Central High. Home of the losers. You, me, and the gimp here."

"Brains will do okay."

"Right. If his old man don't get transferred again." Brains had been to four schools in four years. My parents said his dad didn't get transferred—he just couldn't hold a job.

"Only one thing an airplane is good for," Skeeter said.

Robbie the Runt tugged at my wrist. I turned and looked into his squinty eyes. He said quietly, "You can fix it." His nose was running snot.

"Wipe your nose, Runt."

He stared at me earnestly, swiped a bare hand across his nose, the little Orioles cap he wore in imitation of mine askew on his crew cut. "You can make it fly."

I shook him off my arm. "You're dreaming, Runt. It ain't a model." But I could already see it in my mind's eye: the restored glider, wings bright yellow, holding the sunlight as it swept down the slope on a greased track, then swept through the open gate and lifted into the sky. I watched it soar across the ugly chasm of the borrow pit, a quick shadow darkening the glassy clay pools far below, then skidding down gently into the high grass on the other side.

And that settled it. A bunch of restless boys with all summer on their hands who don't mind stealing lumber and canvas and paint can fix up anything.

What we didn't worry about:

It never occurred to us that the Sparrowhawk didn't belong to us, that we would essentially be stealing it. All of us except Robbie the Runt were already experienced thieves—money from our moms' pocketbooks, penknives from the Western Auto, Christmas ornaments off lawns.

We didn't worry about Old Man Saylor catching us and turning us in to the cops. Nobody had been in that barn in years and years, and from the cover of that thicket surrounding the front of the hangar, we could spot anybody coming literally a mile away.

And one other thing: we never really considered the possibility that the Sparrowhawk glider wouldn't fly but instead pitch into the borrow pit and cartwheel into pieces at the bottom.

But that's all I thought about.

Skeeter was a great scrounge, and he turned up with two old Boy Scout tents and his mother's sewing box to fix the damaged wings. My job was supervising the rebuild. Moe and I stole framing lumber from one of the house-building sites, a few sticks at a time so it wouldn't be noticed, working at night and dragging the heavy pieces down to the pasture in the dark so we could retrieve them in the morning and haul them the rest of the way with the others helping. Moe stole a can of yellow highway-marker paint from his father's truck.

I cut apart the tents and stitched new patches over the frames. It wasn't easy—the fabric was stiff and the needles kept breaking off. My hands were all cut and raw from the stitching. And before we could even do that, we had to shave down two-by-fours using handsaws and planes, shaping the pieces to match the ones we were replacing. Then we rabbetted joints and screwed them together, hoping they would hold. The new wings took three whole gallons of paint thinner, the closest we had to dope. Moe came up with a spool of baling wire so we could re-rig the wing and tail supports.

I took the model from our bedroom out to the hangar and kept it there so I could compare it to the full-sized glider and make sure we were doing it right.

One night, Dad came into our room to say good night and noticed it was gone. "I traded it for a catcher's mitt," I lied, hoping he wouldn't ask to see it.

He said, "I just hope you're not hanging out with that Moe Gargan character. I hear he's been caught stealing again. I don't want you winding up on the police blotter."

I had no idea what the police blotter was, but that was my father's favorite warning. I guessed it was some big book at the police station that listed which boys weren't ever going to amount to anything. You'd go looking for a job ten years from now, and the guy would say, "Can't hire you, son—your name's on the police blotter." Boys whose names were on the police blotter were doomed to sorry, broken lives. Like Moe and Skeeter. And probably me, too. Just a matter of time.

We worked every day, all day, taking time out to wolf down peanut-butter sandwiches and Cokes for lunch, then starting right back in.

Robbie the Runt and Skeeter acted as lookouts. Moe cleared the track and greased it with two cans of Crisco he stole from the

A&P, then cut the chain off the fence gate using bolt cutters he borrowed from his father's workshop.

Brains did the math: what our takeoff speed had to be, how far the Sparrowhawk would glide on a certain wind velocity, how far it would drop. He set up an anemometer, which he had stolen from the high school physics lab, to measure the wind velocity. Skeeter contributed a windsock made from one of his mother's nylon stockings and Moe hung it on an aluminum clothes pole liberated from somebody's backyard, mounted against one of the fence posts at the edge of the borrow pit.

After a few days of calculating, Brains announced, "I don't know if it will make it across."

"What do you mean, you don't know?" Moe asked him.

"What I said, butt-face."

Moe smacked him on the head, the way he was always doing to Skeeter. He didn't to me, because I was almost as big as Moe.

"Cut it out!" Brains said. "Look." He held out a notebook full of equations. Moe and I studied it, like we knew what it said, but for all we knew it could have been a Chinese crossword puzzle. "You don't get it, do you?"

We just stared at him.

"You're too heavy."

"Who is?" Moe demanded.

"You are. And you, too, Marshall. And Skeeter. And me, for that matter. We made the wings too short. The payload has got to be seventy pounds, max. Sixty would be better."

Robbie the Runt, as usual, poked his nose in where it didn't belong. "I'll do it," he said brightly. "I can fly. Marsh can show me how." He was grinning like a moron. "Can't you, Marsh?"

They all looked at me. For once he was right. For once, a runt was exactly what we needed. "Yeah," I said, "Sure, Runt."

THERE ARE MOMENTS IN a boy's life when time stalls and he stands exactly on the verge of who he was and who he is going to be. The light is perfect, a shaft beamed right down from heaven, and even if he is in a crowd, he stands alone. It's as if a chasm has opened up before him, narrow enough to step across, if he chooses to, and if he is sure-footed. But the chasm is also deep enough to swallow him forever if he stumbles. And if he does not step, the chasm grows wider and wider, until he can no longer step across. From now on, all that matters will happen on the other side of that chasm, and he will lose his chance to be part of it.

It is a moment when he must depend wholly on his instincts, his intuition, that little voice inside that will, with the right word, make him a saint or a criminal. He must step across to the rest of his life.

In such a moment I saw Penny Saylor stepping out of the shadows and into the waning sunlight of the summer pasture. I had stayed behind when the other boys went home. For once Robbie the Runt was nowhere around. He'd had to go to the dentist that afternoon to get braces put on his teeth.

She didn't see me at first. She was wearing cutoff shorts and a white blouse, and her head was bowed so that her red hair fell around her face, hiding her eyes. She walked slowly through the high grass straight toward the hangar and stopped when she saw me at the edge of the thicket.

"I thought I saw somebody out here the other day," she said without looking up.

"We don't mean no harm," I said.

"You found the old hangar," she said and kept walking past me through the new entrance we had hacked out of the thicket till she stood inside the hangar. The Sparrowhawk gleamed like a yellow jewel. She laid a hand on one wing, as if feeling for a pulse. "This thing's been out here since before I was even born. My grandfather always meant to try to fly it someday."

"I bet he flew it plenty."

She turned. "No, his boy died. My father. In the war. He stopped coming out here then." She walked to the far door and unlatched it, swung it open. "That awful pit wasn't even here then. It was just sloping pastureland all way across." She swept her hand toward the pit and for a moment I saw what she was seeing.

I wondered whether she would tell the old man, spoil everything. From where we were standing, the rails were plain to see and the nylon windsock fluttered in a fitful breeze.

"Tell you the truth? I think he was glad to have an excuse not to fly it. I think it scared him. I think you'd have to be crazy to try to fly a kite like this."

"I bet it would work," I said, but all at once my heart didn't believe it anymore. All this time, I'd been operating under the assumption that we would only be trying to do what had already been done. But he had never flown across any borrow pit. Never flown at all.

Silence hung in the air like mist. You could touch it and feel it clammy on your skin. Then she looked at me. "You know what I just found out?" she said, looking weirdly distracted and calm.

"What?"

"My husband Bill. He's dead. His car crashed up in Pennsylvania."

I looked her full in the face and saw then that her green eyes were swollen red, that she must have been wandering around the pasture for hours. I had no idea what to say, so I took her hand in mine and kissed it. She hugged my arm to her breast and cried a little, and I was so close, her soft red hair brushed my face. I'd never been this close to any woman except my mother, and it felt so good I trembled.

"It's this farm," she said. "Everything dies here."

The way she said it chilled me to the bone, but I had no idea what to say back.

She turned abruptly and touched the wing of the glider. "I'm glad you painted it," she said. "It looks beautiful. It doesn't look dead anymore." Then she leaned my way and kissed me quickly on the cheek. "Be a good boy," she said, "and walk me back to the creek."

Two days later, on a cloudy Saturday, I watched a procession of cars rumble down the dirt lane to the Saylor farm. The funeral reception. The cars came and went in a pall of July dust, and when they were gone I slipped into the pasture and made my way out to the hangar just to make sure everything was still there. Inside the hangar, in the dusty light, I listened to the first rain splatter against the tin roof. It was oddly comforting. I carefully climbed onto the pilot's cradle and closed my eyes, swaying my body left and right to turn the rudder, hearing it swish behind me, tensioning the levers that controlled the wires and moved the ailerons, the way I had coached Robbie. I imagined Penny watching us fly, her red hair unfurled like a banner in the breeze, her face lighting up with wonder at what we were doing.

But I couldn't hold the daydream. The rain drummed hard on the roof now, and my stomach was all knotted with a terrible conviction. Tomorrow afternoon, we were going to launch my little brother over the side of a cliff and watch him smash to pieces. And that would be the end of the world.

The next day was brilliant and breezy, with high cumulous clouds scudding in from the west. Robbie the Runt set himself in the cradle as he had practiced, grinning though his silver braces. Moe, Brains, and I took up our positions behind each wing and the tail and gently pushed the glider out of the barn into the light.

"You count us down, Robbie," I said.

"Roger," he said. I heard him take an exaggerated deep breath and start the countdown at ten. "Three, two, one—blastoff!" he squealed.

We shoved hard, walked, then ran, still pushing, Robbie prone across the wing. The glider slid down the greased rails, picking up speed. At the edge of the meadow we let go and staggered to a halt on the lip of the borrow pit and the plane kept going. We had done it, launched the beautiful Sparrowhawk into the sky, right off the rim of the borrow pit.

I watched the ground slip out from underneath Robbie, and he was alone in the empty air, frozen, hands gripping the control wires.

Then the glider stalled and dipped toward the faraway floor of the pit and the bottom dropped out of my heart. I caught a breathless glimpse of what it would be like to be free of childhood—the thrill of it, and the terror. I could not have said it in those words then, but that does not make it untrue. Most things that mattered then were far beyond my ability to put into sentences.

Robbie lost his hold, or maybe let go on purpose, and he tumbled out of the sky to the mud-clay flank of the borrow pit and slid all the way to the bottom before he stopped. The yellow Sparrowhawk spun gracelessly in slow agonizing motion into the muddy pool at the bottom and splintered into junk. Robbie lay near it, slathered in mud. His high top sneakers had come off. He wasn't moving, then suddenly he was, scrabbling to his feet, dancing around in the mud, clapping his hands together and yelling at the sky like a crazy boy. He was all scratched up, filthy as a stray dog, but I never saw him so happy in his life.

MOE WAS RIGHT. IT was the greatest thing we ever did. There was no keeping it a secret.

I spent the summer grounded, allowed out of the yard only to deliver my paper route. In a few months, my parents sent me to Catholic high school up in the city, to learn some discipline, they said. What I learned instead was the mystery of books, how to spin thoughts into sentences and not feel so alone in this world. That turned out to be the happy accident of my life, the one thing I never expected. Moe and Skeeter went to Central High and we lost track of each other. Brains' dad got transferred again and he left town forever.

The smashed up Sparrowhawk rotted away at the bottom of the borrow pit, stabbed and broken in the oily water.

The day after the crash, a Wedgewood-blue Ford pickup truck pulled up in front of our house. We were all seated at the supper table, and I could see through the dining-room window two figures coming slowly up the front walk. When the door bell rang, I sprang up and ran to open it. Penny Saylor stood there in a bottle-green dress, her red hair pulled back in a ponytail, her face radiant with grief. Behind her stood a gaunt, bearded man. Her grandfather, Old Man Saylor. He pointed to me and said abruptly, "This the one?"

Penny shook her head.

Old Mr. Saylor squinted his blue eyes at me. "Then you're a little shit."

"Yes, sir," I said, the most honest admission of my life. "That would be me."

"Just don't grow up to be a bigger shit."

Penny pointed behind me to Robbie the Runt, who as always was suddenly jostling at my elbow. My father stood in his suit and tie, a dinner napkin still pinned to his collar. "What's this all about?" He was rattled, caught off guard, and for an instant I wondered if Old Man Saylor was going to sock him for letting his wild boys destroy his beautiful 1912 Sparrowhawk glider airplane.

Mr. Saylor ignored him and reached out a hand to Robbie, drew him outside. "So you're the one," he said softly and bent down closer to him. "You're the ace." He shook his hand theatrically and placed something in it, then he turned without another word and walked back to his truck. Penny glanced back over her shoulder and smiled—at either Robbie or me, I couldn't be sure.

Later that night, when we were tucked into our narrow bunk beds on opposite sides of our room, with the lights out and the streetlight glancing off the ceiling in a little triangle, dad came into our bedroom and threw all the airplane models out the window into the trash can. One by one, he snatched them off their wires and sailed them into the dark, and I think he enjoyed doing it. It was awful to watch. I lay on my bunk bed and stared at nothing and didn't say a word but just listened. You could hear each one splintering as it hit the steel rim of the trash can. He said not a word, but I could hear him choking on his anger, breathing in heavy *chuffs*.

And that splintering sound is the same sound I always hear whenever somebody's dream gets busted.

After he was gone, Robbie called softly, "Marsh?"

"Yeah."

"I can't help it if I like reading books. I don't mean to, you know. Show off."

"It's all right," I told him. "You learn a lot. You know a lot."

"I don't know anything. Don't know as much now as I knew yesterday."

"Don't talk stupid."

It was a hot, humid night, and we lay on our beds uncovered, sweating on the sheets. Those sticky nights always seemed to last forever. Far off, a train rumbled by on the B&O track and let loose a horn blast at the crossing in town.

"Marsh? I've got to tell you something."

"It's okay, Robbie. Whatever it is."

"Tonight? It wasn't the first time I ever saw Penny Saylor."

"What?" I was up on my elbow staring across the dim light filtered by the wavy curtains. Overhead, the empty wires swayed silently, released from the weight of the airplanes they had once held. The dancing wires made it seem like the ghosts of the airplanes were still dangling there in the breeze.

"I came looking for you that day. When she was crying. I heard you talking to her."

So I told him my secret. "Old Man Saylor never flew that glider. You were the first."

"I know, Marsh."

"You don't get it."

"Just cause you think it was a certain way doesn't make it so."

What could I say to the kid? I had pushed him down that track, launched him toward a big hole in the ground. If I was really honest with myself, I knew that glider would never get off the ground. I knew what I was doing to him. Some part of me, the part that inspired such black anger in my father, wanted to watch it happen— the joyful calamity of it, the greatness of the awful thing. I was pretty low-down, all right.

Robbie said, "I was pretty sure, you know, if anybody could. I was pretty sure you could make it fly."

"Pretty sure?"

"Well, if it didn't, the joke would be on you. You'd be on the police blotter forever."

That sent us both into fits of laughing. Jeez, what a dumb puke. What a stupid runt of a kid brother. We were all on the police blotter forever, now.

All the laughter ran out of us after a while, and I was remembering Penny and how I had walked her to the creek that awful day. What I was seeing on her face was more than plain sorrow. It was the loss of hope. The future taken from her. And for just a few minutes, as I held her hand and guided her along the little path and watched her feet stumble because she was crying too hard to see where she was stepping, I was bigger and stronger and better and older than I would be for many years to come, and at least I could hold onto that.

Then I remembered. "What did he give you? Mister Saylor?" I looked across to his bed and he held something up. The streetlight glinted off a little pair of silver wings.

"The real deal," Robbie said, and flipped them across the room. I caught them and was surprised at the solid weight of them in my hand. I tossed them back to Robbie and heard his hand slap around them.

Robbie was a doer after all. He read books not because he wanted to know about Washington and Teddy Roosevelt, but because he wanted to *be* Teddy Roosevelt, to charge up San Juan

Hill. I was the one who watched and never did anything. What did I ever do? The biggest model I ever built nose-dived into the clay pit.

Wreckage, that was all I had ever made. Me. Just a little shit who was probably going to grow up to be a bigger shit. Old Man Saylor's fierce, blue eyes held the truth. I kept seeing him, hearing him say it over and over.

Then after a little while I was crying. Robbie said, "You okay, Marsh?"

"Shut up," I said.

"He didn't get one of them."

"What are you talking about?"

Robbie giggled, whispered, "The Sparrowhawk. The model. It's still out there in the hangar."

The wires overhead fluttered with their phantom wings. "Go to sleep, Ace."

O Canada

Canada was just a place in somebody else's story until Dad pressed a knot of bills into my palm and closed my fist over it with both hands, like it was getaway money. Outside, the yellow Falcon was already gassed and packed with a cooler of Easter ham leftovers and Cokes, and in the trunk were Quebec tags with current registration.

"So you don't stand out," he said.

I was ready to fly up that dark sluice of a highway out of Burlington until the signs turned French and the moon went down, slide east like a raindrop on a windowsill until I found that one secret bootlegger's opening to soak across the border, then run north up those lonely glimmering fields to Newfoundland. It would be a one-way trip.

It was 1971, and I'd been eighteen for three weeks, an only son. I had a scholarship to the University of Vermont, and after that I was on my way to law school. My parents never even went to college. But none of that was worth a deferment: by then, they were taking everybody. The war was turning big, spreading out, craving men.

Two hockey pals of mine were already MIA in the Mekong Delta, one of many exotic place names that were suddenly familiar. Three more guys who had graduated from my high school a year ahead of me were humping it through basic in Missouri, North

Carolina, New Jersey. But they were the dumbshits, guys with no future. Even they knew it. Guys who played catcher and left tackle and goalie and flunked algebra three times. Guys like me didn't go. We used our heads and made our plans and did our parents proud.

Mom circled my neck with her arms, her head pressed sideways into my chest, holding me there. Dad shook my hand and said, "You better get a move on, Sport."

The Falcon was warm, motor running. The old man always took care of me, in his oblique way. I levered the car into gear and pulled away from the curb slowly, turned left at the end of the block and into the sparse traffic, toward Canada.

The evening my draft notice arrived, we three sat around the supper table long after the dishes had been cleared, the way we used to when we had company and the cards finally came out of the drawer. My mother drank tea. She was still pretty, but, judging by photographs, harder now than when she had married. Her face had sharp, Yankee angles to it. The crow's-feet at her eyes and the thin creases at her mouth were not laugh lines. The little fingers around the teacup had the lean, bony strength of years of scrubbing, fixing, hauling, mending. Years with no fat on them.

My father pulled a Labatt out of the fridge and handed it to me—something he had never done before. "You have some choices to make, Sport," he said in an almost offhand way, tapping the envelope on edge. He had a small welding business, and he was a worrier—cranky, easily upset over any little snag. But in a real crisis, he calmed right down, and you knew, whatever went wrong, it wouldn't be because of him.

"I don't know, Carl," my mother said, not looking at either of us. "You went to war. And you came back." She watched his face for a reaction, but my father's face went all stony, the way it did when he was waiting out the bad. "Maybe they won't send him over there at all."

"Over there," he repeated, reproaching her that she could not even say the word out loud: *Vietnam*. My father lit a cigar. He never smoked in the house, only in the garage, but my mother said nothing, only pursed her lips. For a second I was afraid he would offer me a cigar, and I had enough choices tonight without choosing to offend my mother. "We both know better than that," he said, so sure of himself that it scared me. The end of the cigar flared with the suck of breath, and the pungent smoke hung no higher than our eyes.

My mother said, "It's the family I'm thinking of. Maybe you don't have to think of it, but I do."

"Meaning? Go on and say it."

"Meaning, this is one time you can't take the easy way out."

"Don't start that. Are you going to start up with that?"

"You've got to think about what happens afterward."

"You're thinking too far ahead. Way too far." He took a long drag on the cigar and then blew out a plume of dirty smoke.

"It's only for a year, over there. You can stand anything for a year."

"Canada's close," I said, before I had even thought of it. I didn't want them getting into it right now. Anyway, it was my decision, and I had thought about it plenty. From sixth grade on, the war had been a dark certainty brooding over my life, the big awful thing waiting for me just beyond the doorway. It flickered across the TV almost every night, tiger-striped figures hunching toward helicopters, the sound track a steady *pop-popping* of automatic gunfire and the *thwop-thwop-thwopping* of the Huey rotor blades. It invaded my dreams, livid mercurial nightmares of exploding body parts. Many days I felt the fear in my stomach, a cold weight settled there like a bad meal. It was not death I feared but being maimed, not being whole, having some crucial parts of me sheared off in the violent starburst of a booby-trap.

"It's not far," I said "I'd come back to visit." My mother smoothed the auburn hair along her temple. She turned her gray eyes on Dad and they transacted a complicated business between them that had to do with things that had happened long before me. It was one of those terrifying moments when you know you're really growing up, because you can actually envision the world without you.

"So you think like that," she said. "You think like a boy, and I don't blame you." She had that edge to her voice. "But whatever you think you know, you had better know this: if you leave for Canada, you leave for good. That will be your country."

"Catherine, there's no need—" my father said.

"Yes, there is."

"Don't be so dramatic."

"I could sneak back anytime," I said. "Nothing to it."

She shook her head. "The country is at war. You've never seen a war."

"Dammit, Catherine—"

She ignored my father. "Listen to me: Long after this war is over and they're calling them up for the next one, where will you be? Hiding out in some dirty Canuck town, not trusting anybody, that's where."

I just stared at her, unable to stop the sudden torrent of words, as if she had been waiting to make this speech for months, years even—and maybe she had been.

"All by yourself. And every time we go to the Post Office, your picture will be up there on the wall with the others."

"Who cares about the others?" Dad said. "You think I care about the others?"

She turned to him. "They're your people."

"Mom—"

"And if you ever set foot back in town, it won't take ten minutes for them to know you're here. Ten minutes." Nobody said anything.

She left the table and put up her teacup and saucer without a sound, and because my father said nothing at all until the water ran into the cup, I knew we both believed her.

"Let's take a walk," he said and led me out through the garage, so we each could stuff a fresh beer in our coat pocket, and when we were outside, he actually did offer me a cigar and I took it. He showed me how to light it, holding the flame just under the end and turning it round and round for an even burn. I puffed on it and my gums tingled from the bite of the harsh, blue smoke.

It was a damp, chilly time, a week until Good Friday, the crusted, dirty snow still clinging like scabs to the edges of things. It would be another week, maybe two, before the thaw set in, and mud season turned the world to shit. No matter how careful you were, every day your shoes would get caked and the cuffs of your pants would get matted with the stuff. You'd track it into the house a hundred times a day, red glutinous paste stinking of clay. And the long, straight scar of dirt road that ran past the house would turn into a glistering boot-sucking trench.

We drank our beers fast and threw the bottles into the snow, never mind the deposit. "You never talked about the war," I challenged him. His war, I meant. "Is that what you brought me out here for?"

He looked straight ahead, and our boots crunched the frozen ground. "Nineteen forty-two, I was twenty years old. They drafted me into the Marines. Spent six hundred and eleven days in the Pacific." He drew the fresh bottle out of his pocket and popped the cap and swigged from the bottle. "I counted them."

I was thinking of old, gray photographs I had seen. My father, slimmer, a jaunty moustache on his tanned face, standing shirtless in the middle of a group of other men just like him, gray palm trees in the background, autographs scored across his arms, his legs, his bare chest.

"It was different for you." I said. "You had things to fight for."

He sighed and kicked a clod and sent it spinning off into the darkness like a dead planet. "No war is any different from any other war, Sport. That's the main thing to remember."

We weren't walking toward the road, the lights. We were walking the other way, to where the road rose and curved and petered out at the edge of thick woods. Beyond those woods, twenty miles or so, Lake Champlain shimmered in uncertain moonlight, and our little sloop *Sugar Babe*, dressed in canvas skirts, waited out the winter on her cradle at Tynan's boatyard. When I was twelve, I had helped Dad build her out of scrap lumber and nails, and he machined all the metal fittings himself. Everybody in the lake country, rich or poor, had three things: a chain saw, a snowmobile, and a boat.

"Hell, Sport, what do you want me to say," he said after a few minutes of smoking and walking. "God knows, I've never talked to you like I should." And I wondered if we could just go on walking like that all night. Dad was a man who did most of his talking with his hands. For as long as I could remember, he'd been going to his shop six days a week, leaving early and coming home late, every day but Sunday. Love was a handshake and a pat on the back, punishment the hard flat of his hand stinging my backside. Birthday presents were something he made with a welding torch and an electric grinder and left in the garage for me to find: a scooter, a sled, a knife.

"You ever tell Mom about the war?" I asked.

He tossed the second empty bottle off into the darkness. "What would be the point? Women don't fight the goddamn things. Men do." He took his time. We walked. "All the boys in my high school class, Warren Harding High, they couldn't wait. Every damn one of them. I liked it fine right here where I was. But the thing is—" He stopped in the middle of the frozen road, puffed his cigar, and shoved his hands deep into his pockets.

I could see his eyes under the shadow of his brows, squinting hard at me. He waved the cigar at me. "Listen. You know how many Japs I saw? Up close, alive? In six hundred and eleven days? Exactly one. We had taken Okinawa like, a month before. The battle was over. I pulled guard duty. He came slinking into camp in the middle of the night, all brown and shriveled, starved crazy, jabbering away. Christ only knows how long he'd been hiding out in the hills. Poor son of a bitch came down to surrender. It was a big deal."

"You were never in combat?" I had always pictured my father as some kind of gung-ho Marine. I thought everybody had killed somebody in that war.

"That's not what I said. My platoon, our casualties were almost thirty percent. We were always mopping up, that's what they called it. Shooting at rocks and caves, rocks and caves shooting back at us until we got the flamethrowers up. And every time we hit the beach, somebody drowned. Some other poor joker stepped on a mine or got his head blown off by a sniper. And there was the routine stuff—air raids, malaria, dengue fever. All kinds of ways to get jammed up. One guy just disappeared out of his tent. Just wasn't there in the morning. We never did find out where he went."

"This is all news to me."

"It's news to everybody, Sport."

"This isn't what I need," I said. I had no idea what that was, except maybe some way to get from this moment to whatever came next without flying apart.

"You know what we were fighting for?" my father said, like he had just thought of it, or had once known it but had forgotten and only now remembered. "To come home."

The woods were close, a dark loom like ramparts rising up in front of us. There were no lights out here, but moonlight filtered through the clouds.

I wanted to ask him about things: the nights I heard him rattling around downstairs long after I'd gone to bed. About the sharp, mean words spoken over the newspaper on Sunday morning, words meant to hurt. How he hit her once and how I knew it and didn't do anything. They were fighting about me that time, that was all I could tell. I don't know what she said, but I heard the sharp slap of his hand against her cheek and then a big silence. Did he know the things I said to her later? That I told her to leave? That behind his back she still called him a good man and then cursed him?

Did he know how I watched him in the shop just to see him angry—the furious way he'd shoot that blue flame into a steel joint, metal sparks arcing past the blank shield of his visor, the whole job one long tantrum? How the mystery of that great constant anger enthralled me, and how I felt it rising in me, year after year, burning hotter down in the raw pit of my stomach, along with the fear?

I couldn't ask him anything. Instead, he asked me: "Who are you inside?" He looked at me with eyes that looked old and sad. "What you got to ask yourself. That's all."

He stamped out his cigar on the hardpan. "Dead end," he said. "Better turn back." He walked on ahead of me, quickly, the way he had when I was a kid and I was always running after him. I tossed my cigar away still burning and caught up in a few strides. "I'll stay for Easter," I said. "Tell Mom in the morning, after church. I don't want to spoil anything. I'll go after supper."

Later that night, as I lay facing the wall hours after I'd gone to bed, a wedge of yellow light from the hallway painted the wall above my head. I don't know if it was him, or my mother, or both of them, and I waited, unmoving, for the familiar weight on the side of the bed. For the warm hand on my forehead, the soft breath of a mother, a father, come to tuck me in against the chill and the night and bad dreams.

But they hadn't done that in years. The door whispered shut, and I heard tired footfalls retreating down the hall.

THREE HOURS INTO FLIGHT, I was off the main highway now, skating along hilly back roads toward Orleans, a French-Canadian logging town just south of the Line—what we called the border. The road I wanted came out of there. The roads up here were a tangle, just graded hardpan, but I was pretty sure I could find it. In high school, we used to run those roads in old, unsprung Fords and rusty Jeeps and drink beer at the rough bars on the other side of the Line. I knew my way.

I was thirsty for something with a bite to it to rinse the sour-apple taste from my mouth. And before I even pried off the lid of the cooler with my right hand, I knew I'd find it in there: a bottle of beer, cool as a gun in my hand. The old man. I swigged on it as I drove, the border looming out of the darkness. Beyond, all of Canada slept, half a continent worth of sanctuary.

I knew the place, the bend in the road marked by a massive, ice-splintered oak. The plain, white stake at the side of the road shone in the headlights. The border. I braked the Falcon and killed the engine. It was the quiet of a country without voices, from here sliding down into darkness all the way to the Arctic Circle. I sat on the hood and drank my beer, then another. Nobody came along. Nobody was going to.

The moon climbed off over the trees and I sat there.

It was true, what my father had said. But the absolute silence of my conscience told me there was more to it. My belly was full of all the words I never said.

I said them to myself now. It had nothing to do with politics or history or even law school. It was about putting the boat in the water in June and hauling it in October, and in between sailing a lake whose bays and harbors were mapped onto my eyes so thoroughly I could navigate them in the dark. It was about the acrid burn of metal on metal in the old man's shop, watching him join pieces together to make a whole thing. It was about driving Mom down to Church Street on Saturday and being recognized by name at the grocery.

Those people padding past my doorway at night leaving slices of light on the bedroom wall were mine, in a way that foreign seacoast at the end of this road could never be.

I sat on the hood and listened to the wind brushing through the pine tops. The woods were full of restless sounds I had heard all my life. The country was stirring, the low winter was lifting.

Back at the house, my mother would be bent over her crewel, Dad would still be in the shop staring into the flame of his welding torch. By the time he came in to bed, Mom would be long asleep. In the morning, she would rise early and make his breakfast, and after he ate quickly, she would linger over her coffee, making a list of the day's chores. And the silence of that house would go on and on with no one to break it anymore.

I listened to the woods and drank another bottle of beer, slowly, feeling a lightness come into my head, listening to the racket of the woods grow louder. At that moment, the world seemed infinite, and that was strangely comforting. Who knows where clarity comes from, or is it only moonlight that illuminates the border—a threshold you have to step across between this moment and the rest of your life? A soothing calm settled on me like music. The cold lump in my stomach lifted, and I felt my body alive and substantial.

I heard my father's voice again across a great distance, saw again his eyes full of ancient sadness. I knew the answer: I wasn't anybody inside. Not yet. So far I was just a kid scared of going away from home, and that one fear had filled me up. There wasn't room for much else. It was as if the person I was meant to become had been put on hold until this was decided. I didn't know for sure what I believed, didn't even know what I wanted. I only knew what I had, what I could lose. The rest would have to come later, catching up to my father, finding out who I was and what I would finally do and why. I started with what I knew for sure, which wasn't much.

I didn't feel brave. I just felt, at that moment, alone in the middle of the big woods, that it was something I could do. I felt out of place and time, a piece of pure fact in the world—reduced to exactly who and what I was: unformed. Beginning to be a person in this world, with weight and a soul. It wasn't up to me anymore. There was no morality in the moment, no courage or judgment, just a kind of blank honesty. *This is possible now, and that is not.*

Nobody ever fought for anything but the chance to come home, the old man said it. I would go to war knowing that. I would go to war. I would do anything they asked, suffer anything they required. I would kill, if that's what it took. It was a war. And if I was unlucky I might even die. So I must be lucky.

But there were things to settle first, words to be said out loud to one another. There was only a little time left.

I got back into the car. If I did not get lost in the hovering darkness of such a big country, I could make it home by morning.

The Circus Train

Two weeks before Christmas, Tim McCall rode the Amtrak up to Connecticut from South Jersey, where he lived with his wife, Amy, and two boys and made a good living as a financial consultant. He could have flown, but he enjoyed the space and swagger of the train, and as evening fell over New England, all the little villages were lit up outside the window in strings of colored lights, and he felt the soft rushing comfort he knew he would feel racketing through the sparkly winter night.

He had made the trip often while his mother suffered through her long, fatal illness, and his younger brother Matthew yanked him back to handle crisis after crisis—minor run-ins with the police, money problems, drunken accidents.

This time it was his father: emergency surgery for his heart.

In his hospital bed in New London, his father looked fine. Tim was strangely disappointed. "Hi, Pop," he said. "I came straight from the train."

"Hi, yourself, Timmy," he said. He was a big man, even at seventy, and if you didn't know him, you'd have thought he had worked outdoors all his life. But for forty-one years, with time out for the army, he had worked in one of the big insurance companies in Hartford.

Tim had no idea what his father actually did all those years. But Monday through Friday he left the house early and came home

late. He wore a suit and tie every working day of his life, and this
set him apart from all their neighbor fathers, who worked at the
submarine yards across the river in Groton and wore blue overalls
and flannel shirts. His father commuted all the way in from New
London, almost fifty miles.

"Come on, Pop. I came all way up here to be with you."

"All way up here," his father echoed. "Sorry to put you out."

Tim took a deep breath. If his father said another cross word,
he was going to get back on the Amtrak and head south.

"Look, I'm sorry," his father said. "I get cranky, all by myself."
He quickly added, "I didn't mean anything." Absently, he put his
hand flat on the wound over his heart.

It was a sore point between them. Tim was the elder son, and
he had moved away. He came back only when he had to, and, as
the years passed, he came back less and less. Physically he favored
his mother—slighter of build than his father, darker hair going
to gray.

"You seen Matty yet?" his father said. "Driving for UPS now.
Lot of overtime during the holiday season—he's making a bundle."

"Good," Tim said. Matthew always found a soft landing. His
father's old army buddy, Frank Zemanski, ran the UPS terminal.

"You should call your brother," his father insisted.

"Whatever you say." When visiting hours were over, Tim cabbed
it home in the dark, unlocked the old front door, then turned on
the living room lamp. It glowed weakly. His father never wasted a
dime on the electric, and he remembered his boyhood as a twilight
passage through the dimly lit caves of their old clapboard home.

Tim wore thick glasses now, and he always believed that his
eyesight went bad in that dark house, peering through the murky
light of forty-watt bulbs at his algebra homework.

On a whim, he walked up the street to Fielding's Hardware,
open late for the season, and bought a dozen packages of one
hundred-watt bulbs, went home and screwed them into every socket
he could find and turned on every light in the house. He went

outside and stood at the curb admiring the effect. The house glowed like one of the those alien mother ships from outer space.

Back inside, he got his first good look at the place in years. In the relentless glare, the old house looked shabby and dead. The cheap green carpet in the living room was frayed down to its burlap lining. The tan paint on the living-room walls was rubbed gray around the light switches, the enamel chipped off the lintels and moldings.

Tim went to the kitchen to call Amy and say good night to his boys.

NEXT DAY, TIM SETTLED into a routine: visit his father for an hour in the morning, then catch up on his accounts, working over the phone, then, in the afternoon, work around the house until suppertime, visit his father again, and call home before bedtime.

In his father's swaying Buick, he made a daily trip to Fielding's Hardware, hauling home wall paint, a roll of carpet, a bundle of roofing shingles, and boxes of nails.

On his third trip, old Mr. Fielding himself appeared out of the back room. "You're one of the McCall boys," he said and shook Tim's hand heartily. "I remember you. College boy."

"Right," he said. "Tim."

"Yeah," Mr. Fielding said. "Timmy. Your brother Matty, we're on his delivery route."

"How about that," Tim said.

"Hey, you seen what we're raffling off this year?" Mr. Fielding took him by the arm and steered him to the front display window. "Look at that," he said. It was an electric-blue mountain bike, wrapped in red ribbon and a big red bow. Tim bought two chances, one for each of his boys. Still the same price—a dollar apiece.

At Christmastime, Mr. Fielding always raffled off a special toy and donated the proceeds to the local boys club.

"Remember the year the Zemanski boy won?" Mr. Fielding said. "The year we had the circus train? My favorite prize ever."

The year of the circus train, Mark Zemanski and Tim were in the same class in fifth grade and hung around together after school, watching the shipfitters work on submarines across the river. Back then, Mr. Zemanski worked over there, and the boys would try to spot him among the arc welders and riveters and electricians who crawled over the new hulls. Mr. Zemanski and Tim's father had been in the service together in the Pacific War, and the only war story Tim knew about his father was how he got hit by a sniper on Okinawa, and Mr. Zemanski carried him across his shoulders down the mountain to the aid station.

The circus train was a Lionel special model with a silver steam engine, six cars painted red, blue, and gold with the Ringling Bros. and Barnum & Bailey logo, and a candy-apple-red caboose.

Tim was ten years old, and he wanted that circus train, more than he had ever wanted any present for Christmas. He knew his father had bought two chances, one each for him and Matthew. And he knew Matthew thought the train was boring and had said so right in front of his father. Matthew wanted a BB rifle so he could play Davy Crockett.

But as Tim stared through Fielding's window at that circus train, he let it carry him away to a golden world of exotic, far-off places where daring flyers performed miraculous feats high above the crowd, released from the gravity of ordinary life, lifted by the applause of drab people like his father into a weightless realm at the roof of the world where anything was possible.

Circus people, those were his people. That was the train he was meant to ride. Instead he was stuck in a dim house run by a gray man in a suit who did a job so vague it created no picture in the head. Their life was so ordinary, so unexceptional, it hung around his shoulders like a weight of chains.

Tim was a B-minus student. An average hitter on the baseball team. He couldn't sing or juggle, he had no special aptitude with tools or machines, he wasn't particularly funny or talented or remarkable in any way, and he was old enough to be aware that some other people were.

Matthew, for example, had a talent for being liked, again and again, by children and adults, no matter how bad he screwed up.

But Tim, inside his imagination, lived with the secret hope that he *was* somehow special, in a way that would be revealed in due course and all at once, and he waited for the form of his talent to manifest itself in a little miracle while he watched that train go round and round in the window of Fielding's Hardware.

He named all the little silhouettes in the sleeping car windows: the Amazing Arnold, the blind tightrope walker, and the Fabulous Flying Frambonis, the Gypsy trapeze family. Jasper C. Hall the Human Cannonball perused a boxing magazine in his Pullman berth. The Great Gustaf, tiger tamer extraordinaire, stared wistfully out the last window, longing for his native Siberia.

Tim created extravagant histories for them all, imagined the train pulling out of the winter camp in Florida and heading north up the Atlantic seaboard, always by night, the engine wailing out a warning to the traffic on the crossing ahead, then gliding in at dawn to a new circus ground, the roustabouts swarming off the train, the elephants harnessed to the ridgepoles raising the big top, then the steam calliope rolling off the flatcar to lead the grand parade into town.

Tim's father won the circus train.

He knew this because one morning, while his father was in the shower and his mother was cooking breakfast, he took his father's leather wallet off his bureau and opened it to steal five dollars. He wasn't a thief, but Matthew had rifled Tim's wallet and he needed Christmas money. As soon as he saw the raffle tickets, he felt so overcome with shame that he forgot all about the money. But he memorized the numbers.

The local radio station always announced the winning number on Christmas Eve, the winner would call Fielding's Hardware, and very late, Mr. Fielding would secretly deliver the gift to the home of the winner.

After supper on that Christmas Eve, after the Mr. Magoo radio special, Tim heard the winning number announced. His father went to the kitchen and made a quiet telephone call. Tim's stomach was turning somersaults. Just before midnight, his father slipped out. He didn't start the car, and Tim heard him return in a few minutes.

Tim fell asleep with that circus train going round and round in his head.

But in the morning the only presents under the tree were a BB rifle for Matthew, a baseball glove for him, and the usual assorted toys, clothes, and books.

No circus train.

And then the phone rang. It was Mark Zemanski, so excited he could hardly speak. "I got it!" he said. "I got the circus train!"

Tim's father had given the train to Mr. Zemanski.

Now that he was a father with sons of his own, Tim was ashamed to recall how he sulked that Christmas day. He felt he could never forgive his father for having taken his circus train and given it away without a second thought.

Tim imagined his father had left his wallet unguarded on the bureau as a trap, and he had fallen for it, failed some crucial test of character. He imagined his mother had been part of the whispered conspiracy late into the night behind the closed door of their bedroom. "Yes, you're right," she would be saying, "Timmy really doesn't deserve a circus train." And his father: "Since Matty doesn't want it, let's give it to a boy who will really appreciate it. Uses too much electric anyway."

From the perspective of years, it was clear to Tim that their family began breaking apart on that Christmas. That was the last time he ever really trusted his father, the last holiday untouched by bitter fights at the dinner table about Matthew, the juvenile delinquent. Before the new year was out, Matthew would be arrested for vandalism and his mother would be diagnosed with the disease that would take nearly twenty more years to kill her.

Tim had always believed, irrationally, that his whole life, all their lives, would have turned out indescribably better had he awakened to find that toy circus train winding its eternal circle beneath their tree on that Christmas morning thirty years ago.

THE MORNING OF CHRISTMAS Eve, Tim finished repairs on the house. He had painted the walls, painted the lintels and moldings, recarpeted the living room, replaced a dozen bad shingles on the roof, cleaned the leaves out of the rain gutters, and bought and stacked a cord of seasoned oak firewood. He had also called Matthew five or six times and left word on his answering machine to come by, but so far he hadn't showed.

Tim had a couple of hours to kill before bringing his father home from the hospital, so he laid a fire in the hearth, ready to light, then went out and bought a Christmas tree. When he returned, a big, brown UPS van was parked at the curb, blocking the driveway. In the living room, Matthew was sprawled in an armchair by the fire, sipping a can of beer and smoking a cigarette, and his father sat across from him, also drinking a beer.

"Matty built us a fire," his father said happily. "Isn't that great?"

Matthew grinned up at him and held out his hand without getting up. "Hey, stranger," he said. "Help yourself to a beer." He was wearing a pressed, brown uniform.

"Matty knows I like my can of beer now and again," his father said and slurped at his beer. "He came by the hospital and surprised me—hauled me home in his truck. Thought maybe you forgot."

"Yeah," Tim said. Forgot?

"What you got there?" his father said. "Hey, careful not to get them needles all over the floor."

While Tim mounted the tree in a stand in the front window, he could hear Matthew saying, "Place looks good, Pop—you've really kept it up."

And his father saying, "Well, I like to keep it nice for the holidays, you know. Case somebody drops by." Tim was too angry to speak. How could his father not notice? How could he act like this was exactly the way he had left the house, rather than the shambles Tim had found?

When Tim had the tree in place, Matthew stood up. "Got to get back on my route," he said. "Walk me out."

Here it comes, Tim thought: he's going to hit me up for cash. That was usually how their meetings went.

"Relax," Matthew said at the curb. "It's non-alcoholic beer. And put away your wallet. I just wanted to tell you, I'm doing okay now."

Matthew was doing okay, so that made everything okay.

"Glad things are working out for you," Tim said. Twilight was coming fast. Tim could see their breath hanging in the air between them. How could he tell his brother he didn't like him anymore, didn't even know him, that he was just part of an obligation he couldn't seem to shake, that would follow him for life?

Matthew said, "I'm seeing a girl, got a chance at a promotion. I'm all squared away now."

"Good for you," Tim said, but even as he said it he knew it was too easy, too good to last. Some inconvenient night there'd be another phone call from another police station, or another bad night in another hospital, picking up Matthew's pieces.

In the gray winter light, though, Matthew's eyes were clear and steady. He looked smart and pulled together in the uniform. Maybe he was telling the truth. Matthew grinned, climbed onto his high seat, started the engine, and drove away.

LATER, AT MIDNIGHT MASS, Tim and his father sang the old familiar carols and stood around in the cold afterward talking to some of his father's old friends. Mr. Zemanski shook his father's hand and wished him a merry Christmas, then turned to Tim and did the same. There was a deep sadness in his eyes but also something else, a light of recognition, as if he were really glad to see Tim again.

Back at the house, Tim lit a fire, and they sat up drinking hot cider. He could not recall the last time he had sat up with his father, late into the light, when there was nothing wrong, but only quiet and the warmth of a clean home. "Pop," he said, "You ever miss your job?"

"My job?" his father said. "Hated my job. Hated working under those fluorescent lights all day long. Like working under sunlamps. By five o'clock, my eyes are all burning up."

"I never knew that."

"You weren't supposed to. You were a kid."

Tim said, "I never could figure out why we didn't just live in Hartford."

His father poked the fire. "Hartford is ugly," he said. "Who would live in an ugly place? I wanted you boys to grow up on the water."

"So you made the drive for us."

"I made the drive for me," his father said, still poking the fire. "Loved that drive, up the turnpike through all those trees. Loved it best in the fall."

"I never knew any of this," Tim said.

"You weren't supposed to. A man does certain things for his family. He doesn't whine about it."

"Hey," Tim said, suddenly remembering, "we missed the raffle announcement."

"Fielding would have called," his father reassured him.

Tim said, "Pretty generous guy, Mr. Fielding."

His father shrugged. "A man lives in a place, he gives something back."

Tim laid a new log on the fire. "It was good seeing Mr. Zemanski."

His father shook his head. "Never got over his son. I remember when you and Mark used to buddy around together."

All those years ago, Mark had invited Tim over later on Christmas day, and they'd played with his new train, but there'd been no joy in it for Tim, and it wasn't long after that they stopped hanging around together. After high school, Mark Zemanski enlisted in the Marines with Matthew. Matthew was such a good marksman, he spent his enlistment in North Carolina, training other guys how to shoot. But Mark shipped out to Vietnam and only his medal made it home.

"We used to go look for Mr. Zemanski at the submarine yards," Tim said, recalling how they stared across the water into that exciting world of clanging metal and flying sparks where men were building dangerous things.

His father nodded. "The sons of bitches laid him off a week before Christmas. You must have been, what, ten? Year of the big lay-off, they called it."

Without thinking, Tim blurted out, "So that's why you gave it to him."

His father was startled, and it took a few seconds for him to make the connection. "So you knew," he said softly. "It's bothered you, all this time?" He leaned toward the fire.

"Never mind." Tim shook his head and tried to laugh it off. "It was nothing, a toy train."

"You have to understand," his father said, still looking at the fire, not at him. "It was Matty's ticket that won. Not yours—Matty's."

Tim said, "It's old news, Pop."

"I asked Matty," his father insisted on explaining. "He said it was okay with him."

The fire was going good now, and in the firelight and the Christmas tree lights it was cozy and warm, and his father's face looked younger and softer. It was one of those rare moments in life when everything should have been perfect—the light, the peace, the closeness of two men, a father and a son, who had shared a lifetime.

"You had plenty of toys," his father said, not letting it drop. "You were getting a paper route, you could buy your own train."

"I said, it's old news."

"You're a man now," his father said. "Time you stopped worrying about what you were or were not given, and start giving something back."

Tim said, feeling his throat constrict, "I've given back plenty."

His father shook his head. "It's not a gift if you begrudge it."

Tim just sat there, his face stinging.

Mark Zemanski grew up to be a war hero, he thought, and Matty grew up to be a man in a brown uniform who delivered packages at Christmas, and whose gift it was to make the rest of them forgive him, over and over again, and in forgiving him, think better of themselves.

"A gift, it's a little string between people," his father said, threading his fingers. "And all those strings, they hold a place together. Frank Zemanski carried me out of the jungle and saved my leg, and all I ever gave him in return was a train for his kid. We can't give the big gifts, so we give the little ones."

Tim sat there, his neck hot with shame.

Tim McCall had not grown up to be special.

He did not live among circus people.

He handled other people's money, and because they trusted him, he did it as well as he was able. He had grown up to be—like his father, he realized—a gray man. But now he saw his father all those years performing a kind of high-wire act, all alone, without an audience.

"I'm beat," his father suddenly said. "Help me upstairs."

When Tim came back downstairs, Matty was there, lounging in the overstuffed chair. "You put the house in good shape for him." Matty grinned. "Hey, I'm not as stupid as I've acted all these years."

"Do tell."

"Pop and I were talking," Matthew said. "You remember the year Fielding's raffled off that Lionel circus train?"

"The train Pop won?" Tim said.

Matthew grinned again. "Somehow I always figured you knew." He lit a cigarette and took a long drag. "Pop said it was my ticket that won, and did I mind if he didn't give the train to me." He flicked ashes into the fire. "Hell, no, I told him." He took another drag. "Christmas morning, it's not under the tree. Couldn't believe it. Always bothered me."

"I don't get it," Tim said. "You knew he was going to give it to Mr. Zemanski."

"No," Matty said, "No—I'm thinking, he's going to give it to *you.*"

It was like hearing about somebody else's life, somebody he vaguely recognized but didn't exactly remember. "Tell me everything," Tim said to his brother. "Don't leave anything out."

Tomorrow, he would ride the train back to his wife and sons for Christmas, back to the life he had made out in the world beyond childhood, but for now, they had plenty of firewood and all night long to sit up with this stranger he called a brother, to retell the story of their boyhood together, and this time, this time, to get it right.

Death by Reputation

Thursday morning Paul Sartorius awoke to the certainty that something would happen today to change his life. In the steam of the shower, he recalled having the same feeling on the morning of the day he met his wife, Connie, and on the morning of the day she died in traffic, five years ago now, when he'd first taken the archaeology appointment at State University. And that feeling had overtaken him like a virus on the morning of the day his draft notice arrived in the mail.

But the feeling had been present on an equal number of mornings of days on which nothing happened. He shut the water off and toweled vigorously, raising blood to the surface of his skin.

Paul walked briskly the three blocks to campus clutching a hard-used leather bookbag. He gave more attention than usual to his Introduction to Archaeology class this morning. He was a good teacher and a popular one, at ease behind a lectern or stalking the dais in restless pursuit of archaeological truth.

Nothing happened at lunch, except that Dean Willis came by to congratulate him on his book, *The Speaking Creature*, which would assure tenure. In it, he argued that since the australopithecines developed modern locomotive apparatus and articulate fingers long before their brain case increased in size, the evolution of the brain was directly caused by social developments, especially language, an offshoot of specialized sign language and play. After *A. africanus* disappeared a million years ago, the human brain mushroomed to three times its previous size.

"Much obliged," he said to Dean Willis, shaking his dog-eared hand, wondering if this was all his premonition would amount to.

After a review session in his Methods course, he held his office hours, argued range of variation among individuals of the same species with three graduate students, and walked home to an ordinary supper of baked fish, chowder, and beer, and went to sleep early over William Longacre's article in his theory textbook after several glasses of Scotch, which he had discovered while mourning his wife. It was a quiet night, and he decided, as he often had since Connie's death, to sleep in his overstuffed chair by the fireplace among the insulating walls of books and artifacts of days in sere, rock-hard places like Africa, New Mexico, and Arizona: potsherds, human jawbones, fossilized maize, shreds of ancient fabric dyed with blood and plant juice, a petrified wooden club some Plains Paleo-Indian had once used to stun buffalo and wolves.

Or that was his theory, since it as an oddity among other easily categorized artifacts found in the same complex, a kill site in Colorado. The club was found in association with parts of a human skeleton and the bones of an extinct kind of bison, and the supposition was that this particular individual had come to a bad end in pursuit of red meat. Hunting was a dicey business in those days.

He let the fire burn down, snapped off his reading light, and dreamed of nothing.

SHORTLY AFTER THREE A.M., Paul Sartorius killed a burglar who startled him awake and stood in the doorway to his study glazed by moonlight. The draft from the open window woke him, he decided later. The man poised on the balls of his feet, his back to Paul, a heavy crowbar in his left hand. When he turned his head, Paul struck him with the petrified club.

Once, in the head, dead on the spot.

The police arrived so immediately that Paul wondered if someone else had called them first, and they escorted him to the station while their men and the coroner did all the official things that have to be done when one man kills another.

"It's only a formality, Professor," the detective said. He didn't look like a detective to Paul: tall and loose, his face unlined by care, his blue eyes bright behind sporty, wire-rimmed glasses, comfortably well-dressed in a sweater, slacks, and corduroy jacket. More like a writer or a professional man. Still, he was a man acquainted with murder. "He's one we've been after for a long time for a dozen different things. Robbery, assault, the violent stuff. And he had a weapon, correct?"

Paul nodded. The housebreaking tool had already been collected, labeled, and sent to the police lab for verification of fingerprints.

"There won't be any trouble. This is merely to protect you, in case anybody makes any accusations later."

It made sense. Paul said, "I don't mind." He remembered his premonition and wanted to tell the detective about it, but he knew better than to tell people more than they wanted to know.

THE SQUAD CAR DROPPED him back at home a little before six, and the study was full of light. He had bought the house mainly because of all the windows, but now he felt they had exposed him, let in things that were better kept out, and he felt a rush of fear now the danger was past. The place on the shelf formerly occupied by the club was empty—it was evidence, after all.

For just a second, Paul imagined a circle of wolves and other menacing creatures accumulating outside the pale of a campfire, around which squatting bearded men gestured seriously and plotted how to consolidate their tenuous hold on a hostile world.

The window through which the burglar had entered was still open. Paul shivered in the draft and closed it, took a steaming shower, and walked to campus early. He wanted to be walking. He balked at being alone in the house with the enormity of what had happened. He felt no guilt, just that nagging belated fear. He wished he'd had time to mull over his choices and reach a proper, reasoned decision in a matter so grave, but that was not how it happened. He could not say, in fact, what had caused him to act in such an instinctive, violent fashion, and this troubled him.

It seemed to him, in retrospect, that he had not even been fully awake when he laid the club over the man's head. He could not remember reaching for the club, could only recall the rough fact of it dangling in his hand after the man was down, the moonlight lying across him like a sudden illumination of conscience.

He hadn't even seen the man's face, then or afterward, so he didn't have that cliché of memory to haunt him. What, then? He had the unshakable sense of having been plunged into the heart of a mystery as fundamental as religion, and yet the whole thing was a *fait accompli*, nothing to ponder, nothing to solve.

At his office, he left the door ajar and handled a model skull like a baseball, fingering the eye sockets, imagining the impudent hump of medulla oblongata, running a finger along the blade of brow ridge, feeling the smooth globe of the cap where more primitive ancestors had a spikey sagittal crest to anchor the temporalis, a massive chewing muscle attached to the jaw. Larry Thompson, the chairman of the department, slipped in. "God, you're here. I called the house. It's on the radio, Paul. Can I do anything?"

"That was fast." Paul continued turning the skull in his fingertips, searching it like a globe, probing each recess and orifice.

"You don't have to meet your classes today. What have you got? I'll take care of it." His enormous horn-rims made him look like a man wearing a mask.

"There's just the one. I'll be all right, Larry." Today was Physical Anthropology. They were considering the brain case, the *calvaria,* the armored hollow in the skull where impulse and reason resided, often at odds. It had shrunk since Neanderthal, and no one could say just why. Paul had always found the irony reassuring.

"If you need me, stop by. I'll be around all day. We can have a drink later. How about two o'clock?"

"Righto. Thanks." He had the urge for a drink right now. Instead, he scanned the skull with his magnifying lens and watched the imperfections come up: the faults in joining the parts, indentations, bumps, discolorations, the minute violations of the artistic form as the sculptor would have wrought it. Then he gently hammered his fist into the plastic temple and imagined the brain case erupting under the pressure of the club, impulse and reason scattering in an instant like cartoon stars.

In Physical Anthropology, Paul stressed stereoscopic vision, a flattening of the nose, and the enlargement of the brain case as primary adaptations of the savannah-dwelling *Australophithecus africanus*, an upstart lately descended from the trees, and his larger cousin, *robustus*.

"Stereoscopic vision? Like binoculars?" queried a student in the back row.

"Exactly. It allows perspective, especially over distance, and particularly in an environment where depth perception is essential to survival."

"Like in trees?"

"Like in trees. With bad vision, they'd be falling out like so many ripe apples. Olfaction wasn't so important anymore, but good vision was. Vision was all they had, and color, naturally, was a part of it." He thought momentarily of the man he'd killed, silver on black, two-dimensional, the outlines fogged by sleepiness, and later, the study clarified by the morning sun through the windows like a movie finally focused.

"But these jaspers were walking, not swinging from trees." A titter from the back.

"Certainly. But they developed from the most advanced arboreal primates, or so we believe on good evidence. Once on the savannah, *Australopithecus* probably discovered that his highly specialized eyesight was also his best defense against predators. He was virtually helpless, except for his ability to think and see. His olfactory sense had receded, you see, and was far inferior to that of the other savannah dwellers."

"Why?"

"His brain needed the room formerly occupied by the apparatus of a muzzle, or his head would be dangerously large and heavy."

All at once, the class had stopped taking notes, as if it were a decision reached by jury. Paul was baffled, stopped stalking the platform in mid-stride. A girl in the front row, a favorite of his, looked up at him and said, all at once, "Professor, are you going to tell us about it?"

He was stunned. How could he tell them about something he himself felt he had witnessed only secondhand, of which he knew less and less with each passing hour? He shook his head, sheathed his papers, and walked out, feeling somehow accountable to them and having no idea at all of what to do about it.

Paul ate lunch in a sandwich shop off campus, but Harrison, the social anthropologist, found him anyway. "You've broken a taboo, old buddy. But not to worry. The only thing for it is to go get drunk together."

It sounded reasonable to Paul, whose eyes were burning from concentration and lack of rest. His mouth was dry, and his tongue tasted like a foreign object. He left his sandwich unfinished on its platter.

At Murphy's, over their second scotch, Harrison said, "I'm sorry as hell it happened. But don't let it, you know, get to you." Paul watched his eyes, noticed a certain restless excitement there. Harrison leaned in confidentially. "Listen. You may not believe this, but everybody's killed somebody." He swigged the rest of his drink to make the point.

Paul was stunned. "How's that?"

"You heard me, Paul. Everybody. Even me. I shot a Chinese in Korea. I did that."

"Just one?"

"Yeah."

"It's not the same."

"Don't you believe it."

"It was my house. My house."

"You know what I mean."

Paul had nothing to say.

"You need a place to stay till it blows over?"

Paul drank. "No, really. I'm fine." He was beginning to feel the liquor. His headache was gone, his mouth full of saliva, his heart beating normally. "I never knew about Korea," Paul said, for lack of anything better. He resented Harrison for bringing it up, though he was not sorry for the company. Man has always been a social creature, he reflected, organized against the lovers of the primitive night.

"Hell, it's not on my resumé. People expect a certain objectivity, some tolerance."

Paul had no answer for that. Harrison had to get going. Paul wanted another drink. Harrison left a twenty on the table. "Have one on me. Meditate on some Zuni ruins."

Paul didn't watch him leave. His only meditation was Connie, and his grief was that he had loved her more each year since her passing, something he could neither explain nor accept. It had to do with need, he thought, basic things. Without her, his life had skewed far out of balance, for she had been his truing agent, and lately more and more he had immersed himself in his work with all the grim efficiency of a ghoul, a grave robber. But so are all men, he thought: picking through the sacred grave goods of their forebears like dogs, worrying the clean bones with the gnaw of curiosity.

Two drinks later, one of his students walked in. She was one of his brightest. Paul thought it odd for her to be coming to this bar alone.

"Hello, Professor Sartorius."

"Hello, Miss Dubus."

"Oh, call me Andi, please. We're not in class."

"Okay." He did not say, "Call me Paul," and he didn't know why.

"Should I sit here and pretend like I don't know?"

He shook his head. "I could buy you a drink, though."

"Okay, that's nice."

Paul ordered and got an Irish coffee for her.

"I don't mean to take liberties, but you handled yourself very well in class today, considering all you've been through."

"Thanks. Kind of you to tell me." He drank, unsure what to say. What had he been through?

"What will happen now?"

"Oh, I don't know. Some kind of investigation, I guess."

"You're not in any trouble?"

"The detective said don't worry about it."

"That's a relief."

But it wasn't a relief to him. Somehow it should be more trouble to fix. They were all being too easy on him. He looked at her face in a manner he himself would have considered rude, had he been one of the other dozen early patrons drinking furtively in the dim, filtered light.

Outside it had begun to snow, and this helped his mood. He felt that somehow this long moment in his life must be frozen, last long enough to be analyzed to some conclusion. The girl was not a beauty, but her gesture touched him, and her chubby, unformed face held something essentially good. The oversized designer glasses she wore only exaggerated her look of innocence, for they belonged on someone much older. He did not want to sleep with her, except in the way one wants to cuddle a child, a son or daughter, chastely and without words, only nonsensical sounds of love and reassurance.

"I can't really believe what I did."

"You can talk about it if you want, or you can just drink. I know you don't have anyone. This isn't the time to not have anyone."

She was right, Paul knew, only it wasn't the sympathy of an ingenue he needed, but the love of years. "I think I'll just drink, but I don't mind the company."

She smoothed her blonde hair over her temples and adjusted herself in her seat. "Look, here's a story. I met a boy in high school, and we used to make love at the drive-in."

"That's an old story."

"That's not it." She was blushing so that he could hardly stand it. "He never amounted to much. Last I heard, he's still pumping gas back home. But he told me something once, the only thing he ever said that I remember. He said, 'We're the only creature on earth that's ever surprised by what we do.' That's what he said." She drank confidently, as though she had somehow laid the whole matter to rest.

"I don't know if surprised is the right word."

"You know what I mean."

Paul nodded as he finished the drink and, almost before it was drained, ordered another with a wave of the hand.

"You're going to have an awful head tomorrow."

"Tomorrow isn't the problem, dear."

After three more, she said, "One more and then I'm walking you home." It was a small town, everybody walked. "The snow will clear your head."

"Not that." He was getting drunk. He liked the feeling. It somehow relieved him of responsibility, decision, and floated him along as he knew most men floated along all the time. He deserved this one time. He hadn't been stinking drunk since Connie's accident. That time he had fallen and broken his arm and been grateful and ashamed of the cast he wore for six weeks while he continued to belt the Scotch and eat his dinner out of cans blackened on the gas flame of his stove.

The drink came. He faced it with sudden disgust, as if it were medicine, drained it in one swallow, and rose to leave, staggering. Andi held him by the arm, like a little girl guiding her drunken old man home. He almost fell down the steps going out, but she hoisted him with a sturdy grip.

"Surprise," she said.

The sudden cold did clear his head somewhat. It was only a few blocks to his house, and he let Andi handle the complex matter of fitting the key into the keyhole. Inside, she sat him nervously on the couch and loosened his tie. He closed his eyes.

"I can't stay. You realize that. But I only live up the street. My address is here, if you need me." He heard a pen scratching and a paper folded and weighted with a coffee mug on the end table. "Good night, Professor."

Some time after the door had clicked shut, he opened his eyes and realized he had forgotten to meet Larry, hours ago. He put the girl's address in his overcoat pocket, then went outside and urinated in the snow without a second thought, catching the sudden tang of it in his nostrils. Halfway through the act, he realized what he was doing and was mortified. What if the neighbors had seen? But no one was out and about. He watched his breath float for a moment in the snowy light and then walked for hours through brittle cold along snow-slicked streets, careful to watch straight ahead and avoid looking in windows, afraid of what he might see in them.

At the doorway to a tavern he passed a hot-cider vendor and breathed in the aroma of spiced apples. He passed a restaurant venting the odor of hot grease and broiling meat, and the alley nearby exuded the unmistakable smell of bile and human juices. The wind freshened and scoured his face. He felt all the bones in his face and imagined that he must look changed, skin tight and slick and primitive, eyes hard and cold as marbles. He felt several lifetimes removed from the fresh, soft, fleshy youngster who had guided him home with such care and gentleness.

At six A.M. he was still walking. Despite a cold so intense it had frozen brittle the hairs of his nostrils and glazed the water of his eyes like a skin of ice, his head still felt feverish. He remembered little of the night but was alert enough to realize the snow had stopped. He would go and see her.

"Have you got a telephone?" he asked her.

She stood before him in the doorway holding a flannel nightgown closed with one pink hand, smelling of sleep. "I thought you might come over. Come in, I'll put some coffee on."

He dialed Larry Thompson's number and got Larry after a dozen rings. "What's wrong, guy? You in trouble or something?"

"Listen, Larry. You still have that cabin upstate, the one we all stayed at year before last?" It had been a hunting trip, a chance for men to get away from their wives and their towns and drink without glasses and piss outdoors.

"Why? You want to go up there?"

"I've got the weekend. Thought it might help.'"

"You know how to get there? You know the turnoff?"

"I can remember all right."

"Key's in the woodbox."

"Can you let the detectives know where I am? I don't want them to get the wrong idea."

"Righto. Have a ball. Call me if you have to—there's a phone at the lodge store. You going alone?"

Paul cradled the phone without answering and blinked his eyes twice to clear them. The sudden warmth of her house was almost more than he could stand. He still could not feel his toes.

She was at his elbow with a cup of coffee in a handmade ceramic mug. "I'll just get dressed," she said.

"You don't mind?"

"I said it's not the time to not have anyone."

THEY WALKED BACK TO Paul's house. With a courage born of company and light, he entered the place and rifled through his drawers for a change of clothes, a ragg wool sweater and a Greek fisherman's cap he had not worn in years, Christmas presents from Connie. He changed his shoes for boots, found gloves, and they were out of town before he had spoken another word to her, his old Volvo taking the turns nicely, the tricky road an exercise in focus.

It was an hour and a half to the cutoff and twenty minutes more up a steep, muddy track to the cabin. The mud thawed in the sun, and the wheels spun vigorously for purchase in each patch of sunlight, but they made it. In a fit of pragmatism, he had stopped at the lodge store and provisioned them with bacon and eggs, coffee, steaks, beer, and Scotch.

"What are we going to do here?" she said, stepping out of the car into the muddy snow and flexing her back, arms akimbo.

"How should I know?"

He found the key, and they entered the cabin like spelunkers, testing the light, listening for sounds of habitation, stepping as though each floorboard were a trap. It smelled of sweet pinesap, woodsmoke, and damp animal fur. He lit a kerosene lamp and the room illumined like a stage: double bunks along the far wall, wood stove for cooking in the center, fireplace in the corner, table, chairs, cupboards, a threadbare rug. Above the mantel the mounted head and cape of a black bear.

"Cozy."

"Don't get the wrong idea. I don't even know why I brought you. Nothing in my life seems to be following a plot anymore."

In a gesture he did not anticipate, she hugged him hard, tucking her head in so close to his chin that for the first time he was aware of her smell. He liked it, but in this context he was repelled by it, for it was the smell of sugar and milk, a nursery smell.

"Make love to me, Paul. Maybe you'll feel better. Maybe I will, too."

He broke off clumsily and cleared his eyes with his fists. "Let's unpack," he said

"That wasn't the right thing to say, was it?"

"You're a good girl. It's all right." He paused. The last thing he wished to do was to hurt this girl, who wanted only the best for him. The words he had, though, were only the vaguest shadow of what he wanted to say. "It just wouldn't be right, you know? Maybe it was unfair to bring you up here like this. That's not what I meant at all."

Andi had not moved. "I don't mind. I just wasn't sure what you wanted."

"I just wanted . . . company."

"Shall I make a fire?"

"Yes," he said. "By all means." Paul shed his parka and gathered the ragg wool sweater around his shivering body in bunches.

Hours later, they sat before the fire with a single blanket draped across their shoulders and a good meal heavy on their stomachs and sipped Scotch from the bottle. Outside the snow had resumed, tentatively at first, then with real, bewildering force. The winds swept over the roof like surf and broke with the same thunder, wailed around the chimney top and occasionally blew up a starburst of cinders in the hearth.

Paul held the poker in his hand. The end of it glowed from the heat. His hand trembled with the weight of it, and he allowed the hooked brass tip to rest in the embers. It seemed after a few minutes so heavy he could not lift it again in this lifetime. Outside he imagined animals snowbound in their dens or prowling for prey, badgers and weasels stalking the nighttime killing ground among the black posts of pine and spruce, moose and deer and bear safely bedded down in windless places snug enough to hold their warmth, all they had of life.

In his mind's eye, the steep forest was a negative, the air silvered with snow, all else only shadows, with no weight or substance.

BY MIDNIGHT HE KNEW they were cut off, the precarious road up from the highway a long warp of drifted snow, and he breathed easier. The blizzard descended upon them like a living thing, pounding at the walls of the world and threatening to break through at any moment. In the old days, Paul knew, such a storm would have made men pray.

He thought again of those bearded forms crouching at the edge of light and arguing, as men and only men will do. He imagined their passionate voices rising with the wind in shrill dissonance as the argument heightened, and the danger moved in furtively from the hills, the woods, the shrouded mountains where other deadly creatures lurked, their progress steady as rain, their brains blunt as cobbles, their collective will inevitable as weather, waiting their turn.

Paul longed for Connie, and he had only this girl, this amiable child, who was not his mate. The snow continued. He listened. He rocked her in his arms. He watched the fire and waited. The light of the flames betrayed his vision, and the heat pressed the bones of his face like fingers until he could no longer feel his skin, only the hot rings of his eye sockets and the dumb gape of his mouth. For hours, he listened to it gathering outside.

He ought to be hanged, he knew now. He was a murderer. He understood at last why the club had been so anomalous, what had been the fate of the Indian hunter whose disarticulated bones had been catalogued with it. The thesis was so simple, so naturally elegant, that Paul could not quite believe he had missed it all these years. It was not play, not even language, that had bloated the brain of *Homo sapiens* like a tumor.

They had all been too easy on the beast.

Docile, uncompetitive man would never have needed to rise so high, to be so smart, to achieve such social complexity—tact, gentleness, the ability for fierce love and loyalty. Nothing like a social imperative had selected for cleverness, cunning, ambition. For the hunger to invent words and tools, tribes and religions. For will. He conjured again the ring of men around the open hearth, watched them waggle their frail, flinted spears, listened to their yabbering voices. They were bickering over meat. In an instant of inspired prescience that would assure the survival of his kind, world without end, the shrewdest of them discovered murder.

So that was it. Paul hunkered in front of the fire and waited. When at last she had fallen asleep, he banked the fire, tucked the blanket around her pliant shoulders, and stood shirtless at her back. Then he slipped into the thick ragg wool sweater, put on his hat, and stepped outdoors.

The air was thick with night smells: the bite of woodsmoke, the tang of pine boughs, the sting of snow. The wind had slacked, and the snow sifted down through the barren branches gently, like dust, layer upon layer, lens upon lens, like the amber seal of history. It drifted high around the foundations with a soft rattle, settled ever deeper on the lost road, powdered the brim of Paul's cap with a residue of fallen light.

He stared up into the black trees, blind, in his quickening man's heart the rapture of fear, the thrill of recognition, the blessed weight of choice.

Flexible Flyer

To wish for a sled for Christmas was to wish for two nearly impossible things to come true at once: an expensive gift at a time in our family's life when my parents were barely holding their own, and snow. Where we lived, it almost never snowed.

We studied pictures in our geography books of snow—drifts that buried automobiles in Buffalo, blizzards that swept across the Great Plains, heaping snow against fences and barns, New England snows that turned farm lanes into postcard trails for horse-drawn sleighs.

But in Delaware, our home, we never got real snow. A dozen flurries a year. Once or twice, a couple of inches that would turn to slush or get sluiced away when the weather turned warm and rainy the following day.

My little brother Nick wanted a sled.

He'd found a picture of one in *Boys' Life* magazine—two happy scouts screaming down a snow-covered hill on a gleaming sled with shiny steel runners. The logo streaming across the bottom of the advertisement read: *Flexible Flyer Racer*.

"That's the ticket," Nick said. We were sitting side by side on the couch in the basement rec room watching *Sergeant Preston of the Yukon* on TV. Sergeant Preston's giant Malamute, Yukon King, was chasing some bad guys through the snow, breasting through the drifts with his powerful chest, spraying surfy clouds of spindrift.

"You're too young for a sled," I told him. "You're only six." I was ten. Between us we had a sister, Molly, who was eight.

"Seven, almost," he said. And he was right. His birthday fell on the day after Christmas, a really lousy time for a kid to have a birthday. I mean, you were practically sharing it with Jesus. And no matter what our parents did, even Molly and I had to agree that Nick always got cheated out of a real birthday with a party and cake and amazing presents.

"There aren't any hills around here, Nick," I said. "Where you going to ride it?"

"On the church hill," he said.

Again, he was right. St. Stephen's, our Catholic church, stood at the pinnacle of a long, gentle slope outside of town in what was still considered the country. The road ran several miles up the hill past cornfields and pastures to a cleared lot tucked into the side of the woods where the old church had been built of pasture oak and fieldstone half a century earlier.

"Okay, so there's one hill, Nick. But there's no snow."

On TV, Yukon King had captured the bad guys, dunked them headfirst into a snowbank, and stood grinning for his master. Every episode ended the same way. Sergeant Preston always got his man.

"It might snow."

"What makes you think it's going to snow?"

"But it might. It has to snow sometime."

"Okay, okay. It *might* snow."

"So I want one. A Flexible Flyer." He sat there with the magazine in his lap, his legs splayed, and stared at me, his pale freckled cheeks reddening, blinking his green eyes fast, the way he always did when he was getting ready to cry. He took after our mother in looks and had her stubborn streak, too.

"Okay, Nick," I said. I didn't have the heart to say anything else. I grabbed his legs and squeezed them just above the braces and he giggled like he always did. He liked for me to rub his legs because they cramped up and went all spastic if he sat too long. My mother

used to sit for hours every night and rub his legs while Nick bit his
lip and grinned—with the pain or with how good it felt, I could
never tell which.

That was the real reason Nick was crazy to want a sled: He was
a cripple. My mother forbade us to use that word, *cripple*, but that's
what Nick called himself. One day last summer, Nick came back
from the YMCA swimming pool and lay down for his nap. When
he got up, he couldn't walk.

Polio, Doctor Everhart pronounced.

This was the time of Polio, and that was the summer it came
to our town. Doctor Everhart whispered the word, shaking his
head, looking around to make sure it didn't escape from the upstairs
bedroom Nick and I shared. Polio was an evil spell—invisible and
deadly. It could seep through walls and closed doors and strike
without warning, and it nearly always struck kids.

Nobody seemed to know what caused it, or how to cure it. It
came out of nowhere, struck at random, lurked in the shadows of
kids' bedrooms like the bogeyman. People treated it like the black
plague—it was believed you caught it in crowds from bodily contact
with other people. From breathing their bad, poisoned air, or
brushing against their clothes, or swimming in the same water.
Some people claimed that it only struck down the bad kids, but
that was crazy. Being good was no defense. When somebody in
your family caught it, the neighbors' kids stopped coming over to
play. People avoided you at the supermarket. "Polio," they said
knowingly, and pointed, and the other person would nod and frown
and duck down the produce aisle.

We wanted to grow up fast, to outrun Polio.

Doctor Everhart couldn't predict if Nick would ever walk again.
There was no miracle cure, no magic operation. At least Nick wasn't
forced to live in an iron lung, like the boy in our fifth-grade reader.

Nick's legs were strapped into metal braces—he called them
his *Frankenstein legs*—and he propped himself up stiff-legged
between kid-sized crutches that made his shoulders hunch up and

his red, crew-cut head bob forward. He fell a lot, and we got used to the sound of his clattering braces and his crutches rattling against the slick linoleum floor of the kitchen and Nick hooting with pain and laughter. He was always bruised and sore, but he didn't complain much. He just sort of banged his way through the world and hoped for the best.

That summer, Nick wasn't the only kid strapped into steel leg braces.

In our small town that summer, people stopped going to the movies. The YMCA pool closed, as did all the public pools. Nobody gave birthday parties, and the church day camps shut down for lack of attendance. Brides postponed their weddings indefinitely. When school started, half the kids stayed home and nobody got in trouble.

People even stopped going to church. Not our family, though. My mother, who was second-generation-immigrant Irish, said, "We won't turn away from the Good Lord now, just because he's given us a trial."

But Sunday after Sunday, the pews were mostly empty, and Father Cruikshank's ringing sermons echoed in the empty space. At the early Mass, there were always a few crones in the back row, dressed in shapeless black smocks, their heads swathed in black veils so that they were indistinguishable from one another, faceless and bent, clicking on their rosary beads and silent except for their mumbled chant of Latin responses to the priest. By now, I was one of only a handful of altar boys who would still serve Mass.

The Sunday after Nick told me he wanted a Flexible Flyer, two weeks before Christmas, I kneeled on the hard stone at the foot of the altar answering Father Cruikshank's cues: He would say, *Introíbo ad altáre Dei*—I will go in to the altar of God—and I would respond, *Ad Deum qui laetíficat juventútem meam*—The God of my gladness and joy.

But I didn't feel very glad—I felt mad at God for what he had done to Nick and scared stiff it would happen to me. I shared a room with him, I rubbed his legs every day, I breathed his air. I rattled off the Latin by heart, thinking of Nick and his lousy braces and how he wanted a sled, the stupidest thing in the world for a cripple to want in a place without hills or snow.

I didn't have to turn around and look to see Nick in the front pew, where our family always sat because my father would have it no other way. "If I'm going to church, I want to see and hear everything that's going on," he always said. Nick's red buzz cut would be shining like a light bulb. His crutches would be stacked against the front rail of the pew and Molly would fidget beside him, her brown curls bouncing each time she wagged her head. On one side my mother, small and wiry, red hair pulled back tightly into a bun, a small, dark-green hat pinned to her head, my father in his charcoal suit, only a little taller, motionless, completely absorbed in the Liturgy, watching it transfixed the way he watched a baseball game or the six o'clock news—as if he were seeing it for the first time, and at any moment something wonderful might happen and he didn't want to miss it.

I was so distracted, I missed my first cue for ringing the bell and later almost dropped the wine cruet, and tall, heroic Father Cruikshank leaned down to me and squinted and said, "You all right, son?" Like I might have suddenly been stricken with Polio, too, and I wondered for a cold split second if I had and that was why I was so clumsy, but I nodded yes.

After Mass, Molly and I held a powwow and decided we would all ask for the sled together. "It's what Nick wants," she said blithely.

"It's a stupid idea," I warned her. "It means you won't get a bike."

"I don't think I'm getting a bike anyway," she said, flipping her curls. Molly was always blasé about herself, like she would get along fine in the world and why did the rest of us worry so much about every little thing? We didn't know much about money in those days—I have no idea even now what salary my father earned from the clothing store he and my mother ran. As bookkeeper, she took no salary, I do know that. And business had fallen off—people just weren't going out anywhere, even shopping, unless they had to. They were hunkered down in their homes, doors and windows shut tight, trying to keep out Polio.

Molly and I went to our parents together, as a kind of delegation, and told them: "We want a sled."

My father said, "Do you have special information I don't? Because, Buster, the last time it snowed enough for sledding, you weren't even born yet."

"Just in case," Molly said with an offhand logic. "Sooner or later, it's got to snow, and when it does, we'll be ready."

"I thought you wanted a new bike," my mother said. "Something you can use every day."

"No, we want a sled," she said, as if it had been so obviously true for years that only a moron would think different. "A Flexible Flyer." She held out the picture, scissored out of *Boys' Life*.

That night, I could hear our parents downstairs in the kitchen. Sometimes they'd sit up after we had all gone to bed and sip coffee at the Formica table and talk about the store, or the news, or things they remembered from when they were first married. I used to like listening to them talk like that, private and low, but sometimes too it reminded me that they had once lived in a world that didn't include us, and I would lie awake scared of something I couldn't even name.

"I don't know if we can even get one this late," my father's voice said.

"I called Western Auto—they can have it by Christmas Eve."

"What in God's name are they thinking? The radio is calling for rain all week. They'll be so disappointed—"

My mother's voice said, "Oh, for the love of Jesus, just buy them the adjectival sled. It's Nicky who wants the thing."

"Nicky? What use will it ever be to him."

On Christmas Eve, it was tradition that we all went to midnight Mass. We piled into the old green Buick and drove up the hill to St. Stephen's in a cold drizzle. I don't remember a gloomier ride than that Christmas Eve ride in the caravan of headlights and taillights crawling up the long hill in the rain, the fields on either side of us dark, nobody talking, not even the radio on to play Christmas carols.

I was serving the Mass with Donny D'Onofrio, so as soon as we hit the parking lot I scooted out and scrambled into the sacristy by the back way and buttoned on my starched cassock and slipped the bleach-white surplice over my shoulders and Donny let me light the candles, which I always enjoyed. I genuflected at the foot of the altar and lit the two golden candelabra and then the special candles next to the Nativity scene on the left side altar, under the statue of the Virgin Mary. In front of the Nativity scene burned a whole rack of votive candles, flickering red—one of them, I knew, my mother had kept burning for Nick ever since July.

At special Masses, Father Cruikshank liked to enter from the front door rather than the sacristy and march up the aisle. So when he was all robed in his vestments, we slipped out the back and walked outdoors to the front of the church and I felt the rain turning to sleet on my cheeks and dabbing my hair, and my surplice was spotted with dark blotches in the floodlights. The lights reached down beyond the parking lot to the edge of the meadow that sloped down alongside the road toward town.

As we entered the front door, the congregation turned to watch us process up the aisle. For the first time since summer, the church was full. And in every pew, it seemed, there were kids in steel leg braces. Crutches—dozens of pairs—leaned against the backs of the wooden benches in front. Other children were laid across the benches, swaddled in blankets and car coats, unable even to sit up.

As he passed each pew, parents stared at Father Cruikshank accusingly for some answer he didn't have, their faces white and their eyes dark with fatigue. There was none of the usual shuffling and coughing and throat-clearing. There was something frozen about the way they looked, all those grown-ups with the damaged children they could not protect.

We sang "O Come All Ye Faithful," even the Latin verses, and Donny and I served the Mass without a hitch. We sang the other carols, but there was no choir—they had stopped rehearsing in the summer for fear of Polio—and the singing was ragged and off-key with the organ. Father Cruikshank read the St. Luke gospel of the Bethlehem story and he did not read the Matthew gospel, which tells of Herod seeking out the young children of the region and putting them to the sword. I don't even remember his sermon. Only about half the congregation dared take communion, and, by the end of Mass, everybody was itching to leave.

I looked out across the congregation—they had all sat too long in a crowded place, a place of danger. Now they did shuffle and cough and clear their throats. They didn't look at their neighbors. They huddled their own children between them. When Father Cruikshank pronounced the final blessing, they sprang up like pop-up dolls. We processed back down the aisle, feeling them crowd along behind us. And when Donny D'Onofrio and I flung open the big double doors, outside was a howling blizzard.

The air was wild with snow, blowing so thick you could hardly see the cars in the parking lot, all layered with white.

The earlier rain had frozen under the snow, which made it impossible to walk on the pavement without falling. Men wearing street shoes with slick soles and women in high heels lost their footing and grabbed each other's coat sleeves for support.

The D'Onofrios herded their five kids into their new Ford and tried to make it down the hill ahead of the rush, but only a couple of hundred yards down, the big car slid sideways into a ditch, and Mrs. D'Onofrio fell hard while getting out. Mr. D'Onofrio sent Donny back for help—he ran through the corn-stubble drifts and reached us out of breath.

My father said, "Come with me."

Slipping and sliding, somehow carrying Nick between us, we followed him to our Buick, and he opened the trunk with a brass key. He reached in and pulled out a long flat package wrapped in red paper. "Go ahead and open it, Buster," he said.

"Let Nicky," Molly said, and Nick hooted and clawed at the paper while we held him upright. In the floodlights, the banner was bright red against the varnished blond wood, the letters glossy black: Flexible Flyer.

"I need it to help Mrs. D'Onofrio, all right?" my father said.

Nick nodded, smiling big.

"For now, everybody go back inside," my father said. "Nobody's going anywhere until the plow comes."

So it was that my father and a few of the other fathers trudged through the snow across the road to the D'Onofrios' car and laid Mrs. D'Onofrio on the sled and hauled her up the hill and back into the church. Her ankle was broken clean, Doctor Everhart said. They laid her in a pew on a pile of coats, and everybody else made themselves comfortable back in the church. They tried to call into town, but the phone line was already down.

Soon after, the power went out, too, so we had only candlelight that played on rows of grim faces. A few people whispered—a muffled complaint, a quick biting hiss to hush a cranky child. Then Father Cruikshank announced it was all right to talk if we did it respectfully. Father Cruikshank sent me and Donny D'Onofrio to get more candles, and we lit them all along the main aisle and by the front doors and around the sanctuary, and the dancing shadows they made were like a whole world of other people, not us—dark, humped figures afraid to stand straight and face each other.

The air smelled like wet wool and beeswax. A man I could not see said to his wife, "I told you we shouldn't have come tonight."

She said, "Don't even start."

Another man said, "Get over it, pal."

A woman started crying softly and her husband cursed and then tried to put his arms around her, but she pulled away. Other voices complained now, murmuring in that low, ugly way of people getting ready to do something stupid that they'll regret. It was the first time I felt ashamed of being in church.

Father Cruikshank stood at the foot of the altar and raised his hands. I stood close enough to touch him. He was lean and darkly handsome, and his voice had an anger in it, just barely. "Stop it, please—it's not the snow. You know what's wrong." He paused. "The thing we never dared speak about."

Somebody in the back called out, "Let it be, Father."

Father Cruikshank faltered—no one had ever dared talk back to him in church—then started again. "I know this is not the kind of Christmas you wished for. Prayed for." He glanced toward the Nativity scene and then looked back at the sullen congregation. He waited for their murmuring to die down, and it took a long time. "What has happened here, this has never happened before. Sometimes—sometimes we're at a loss."

He stopped talking and everybody waited now, quiet. Usually he could speak for an hour without stumbling, but now he groped for the words. His voice went soft, but everybody was listening now, so it didn't have to be loud. He looked at me, as if I could tell him what to say next, but I didn't have a clue. All I had running through my head were those memorized Latin responses, so I said stupidly, "*Ad Deum qui laetíficat juventútem meam.*"

Father Cruikshank frowned, puzzled, then took a slow step toward them. "We are forgetting—we are forgetting the *joy.*"

A man in the front pew put his face in his hands, and his shoulders shook like something was wrong with him.

"We're not sure. Not sure if we still believe. How can I say this?" He scanned their faces, looking from one to the other, seeing just blank, unforgiving stares. His neck was crimson with anger above the pure-white alb. "Today we celebrate the birth of a child. When a child is born, that's the miracle. Always. Then, later—it's true—the child suffers. That's the world."

He lifted both of his big hands and ran them over his face, like he was washing it. "But the suffering is not all there is." He shone his eyes over them like trying to light up a dark place with a small flashlight, like he wanted to find one face in which he recognized faith, and he settled on my mother. She stared back at him hard, and I could not read what was in her heart. "There is also—there is always the joy."

There was utter silence then, like they were waiting for him to say more, but he had no more to say. Some of the parents looked down at their laps. One man got up and clomped loudly down the aisle and out into the snow, and I wondered if others would follow him, but nobody did. They hunkered down in the pews just as they had in their homes, not brave or burning with faith but just tired and wanting to go home, and maybe ashamed.

Father Cruikshank walked slowly back to the sacristy to change out of his vestments. He held his head up, as he always did, but I could tell it was a struggle, that this night had cost him something.

He did not have the power to fix what was wrong, but he had broken the spell. The silence lasted until he was out of sight and for a minute or so longer. Then my mother started whispering to another, asking what she had been doing since summer, and after a few minutes, some of the other women gathered timidly in a little knot near the side confessionals and talked first in halting whispers and then in regular voices about what the doctor had told them or what they had read in a magazine or what they planned to resolve for the New Year. And somebody started crying, and somebody else reached across and patted her arm and said, "There, there."

A couple of men excused themselves to use the restroom in the sacristy. Even with the heat off it was warm enough to take off our heavy coats.

To pass the time, Mr. D'Onofrio suggested we sing Christmas carols, and he started off the first verse of "It Came Upon a Midnight Clear" in a fine tenor voice. At first people sang softly and a little embarrassed, then a few started to sing loud and even smiled at the old familiar words. It was not very good singing—half-hearted and a little off-key—but I heard my mother's soft, melodious trill and my father's flat baritone. We sang only the one carol, as if that was all we had in us.

All the while the snow came down outside, thick and hard, and the wind rattled the windows and drafted in every crack in the old church, flickering the candles.

And soon enough people started sacking out on the pews, cuddling up with their kids and babies and loved ones and closing their eyes, snoring, breathing the deep peacefulness of sleeping in a blessed place. Molly said, "It's like we're pioneers, all gathered in the fort so the Apaches can't get us."

Nick giggled and said, "Or the Devil."

Father Cruikshank in his long flowing cassock patrolled the aisles like a real father, watching over their sleep. The fluttering candles made shadows across the walls and lit up eerie slivers of blue and red and gold in the stained-glass windows.

Outside the snow came down like the blazes all night long. Father Cruikshank went out in back of the sacristy to smoke a cigarette, which he always did after Mass. When we were sure our parents were asleep, Molly and I gently nudged Nick awake and I rubbed his spastic legs for a few minutes, and then between us we carried him outside, where our Flexible Flyer stood propped against the stone side of the church.

At the far end of the building, we could see Father Cruikshank standing in a corner out of the wind, smoking his cigarette. He looked our way and nodded and let us be.

I shook the snow off it, laid it down on its shiny runners, and set Nick aboard with his feet stuck out in front. Molly squeezed on in front of Nick so he could lean against her shoulders. Slipping and sliding, I hauled them across the parking lot to the edge of the meadow, where it sloped down along the road, pure white, and the sky glowed from the snow light. I climbed on behind and tucked my feet into the steering paddles.

The rest of our lives opened out ahead of us full of trouble and heartbreak, we knew that, even as kids we knew that, and tomorrow and for years to come, Nick would wake up with legs iron-stiff with pain, and there would be no Christmas visits, and my mother would cry herself to sleep again.

But this night, a field of unbroken snow spread out before us. Far below, we could see the bright headlights of the snowplow grinding up the hill to rescue everybody.

"How did you know, Nick?" I said, and he just giggled and caught the falling snowflakes on his tongue. Then I pushed off with my hands, hugged Nick hard, and we went flying down the snowy hill.

This Is the Story I Want to Tell

I.

All that happened on a sunny Saturday in July was this: Dan Johnson came bounding down the stairs and into the kitchen very early and announced he was taking the whole family to the beach. He had a kind, slack face with lively eyes, and his dark hair was thinning to a peak in front. Irene, Mrs. Johnson, sat over her coffee, looking a bit secondhand. It was already hot in the kitchen, and she was facing another dreary day of laundry and housework. "I mean it," Dan said. "Ocean City. We can be there in two hours."

"Fine," Irene said. Her hand went distractedly to her auburn hair, coiled carelessly on top of her head. "Let me fix myself."

Tommy, eight years old, clattered down the cellar stairs to retrieve the big, green Coleman cooler. He found it on a shelf, lid propped open, and removed a large wolf spider from inside. He lingered in the cool cellar, watching the hairy spider retreat into a crevice in the dirt floor. Tommy liked to play in the cellar in summertime, pretending he was buried alive, the victim of a mad scientist's revenge.

But he never went down there after dark. At night, Tommy was sure, something else lived in the cellar. He would lie in bed and imagine it slinking out of the crawl space in the damp wall, then resuming its canine shape and stalking to the foot of the stairs below the kitchen, where it would poise on shaggy haunches, panting, its milky, night-seeing eyes fastened on the crack of light under the door, waiting.

Tommy was a runt and had no friends in the neighborhood and lived mostly in his head. He carried the cooler upstairs.

Little Martha, five years old, plastic pail and shovel in hand, stood looking out the kitchen window, and said, "A man is coming."

Irene ignored her and filled the cooler. Her hair was now neatly combed back in a ponytail, and she wore eye makeup.

At last, everyone was ready. Dan opened the door and there stood a tall, ragged stranger in muddy boots, holding a rake. The man was unshaven, with deep-set eyes and a high forehead under a black slouch hat. The hands on the rake were enormous and red. He held it as though he feared someone would try to take it away. His high rubber boots were caked with fresh mud. "Oh!" Dan said, and stepped back. "What can I do for you?"

Tommy stood next to his father and watched the man's slow, watery eyes. "I work," the man said in a voice heavy with some Gypsy Balkan accent.

Dan just stared at him.

"I work," the man said again.

"No work." Dan found himself mimicking the man. "Going to beach."

The man shook his head. "Bad day for beach," he said, pronouncing it *bitch*, and pointed to the leaves that had lain in great clumps all over the yard for many months. "No good for you. I rake."

Dan was stymied. "Tomorrow, come back tomorrow. Work then."

After a few silent moments, the man nodded stoically and plodded next door to the McPhersons', leaving great muddy boot prints across the lawn.

They all got into the car.

Tommy had brought along a Hardy Boys mystery to read. Frank and Joe Hardy were in a secret tunnel. They found cannonballs and an old Confederate map left by a dead courier from Gettysburg. Somebody else was in the tunnel with them, out to foil them, but they didn't know who. Whoever it was kept shadowing them. They heard his muffled footsteps, felt him near, but whenever they turned their flashlights on him, he disappeared. "The kind of spook you only see out of the corner of your eye," Joe Hardy said. It was good stuff. The brothers could always trust each other in a tight spot. Irene kept checking her makeup in the mirror on the back of the sun visor.

"For heaven's sake," Dan said, "stop fooling with yourself."

"Leave me alone," she said. "I want to look nice."

"You look just fine."

"I'm getting old. I sit around the house all day and get old. It's no fun for a woman to get old."

"Oh, for Pete's sake, don't start up. You look just fine. I can't wait to see you in your suit."

"I don't have any tan."

"You'll get one today. We'll have a nice time."

"I'll burn." Irene blew her nose and settled back to enjoy the ride. Less than an hour to go.

Joe and Frank Hardy were in the secret tunnel, and the cannonballs turned out to be painted gold balls. It figured. Tommy admired Joe and Frank for figuring that stuff out. You couldn't figure that stuff out on your own. Meanwhile, the sinister presence in the tunnel was closing in.

A little while later, nearly out of gas, Dan pulled into the first station he came to. Irene got out to use the restroom, and the kids stayed in the car. No attendant came out, so Dan filled the tank himself and went inside to pay, but nobody was there. Nobody at all. The air conditioner hummed, and the radio behind the counter was playing a song about a voodoo lover of the bayou selling cats and teeth and hair.

"Hello?" he called. Nobody answered. He opened the door to the garage and looked around. There was a splash of red paint on the floor and lots of grease. He wouldn't go in there, not wearing white deck shoes. "Hello?" he called, but still nobody answered.

Irene came back around front. "The restroom's locked—can you get the key?"

Dan counted twelve dollars onto the counter and told Irene to get in the car.

"What's going on? I have to use the ladies' room."

"There's nobody here, Irene. Just plain nobody. It isn't right."

So they got back into the car and tried to think no more about it. Instead, Dan thought about the man with the muddy boots. Maybe it *was* a bad idea to go to the beach today. But it had perked Irene right up. She needed to get out more—he kept telling her. Lately, around the house, she was looking like hell.

Dan drove them over the causeway and down a side street where he parked in front of a meter. He put in plenty of quarters, and the four of them carried the cooler, blankets, towels, toys, and two folding chairs across the boardwalk onto the beach. They got settled. "Ain't this just the life," Dan said, snapping the top off a can of soda. "Wonder what the poor folks are doing today."

Tommy lay across the towel on his stomach reading. Little Martha played in the surf with her pail and shovel. Irene spread lotion all over herself. Dan did her back.

"Smells just like coconuts," Dan said. "You're a goddamned coconut!" He laughed, feeling jaunty.

They nibbled on pears and tomato sandwiches and lost track of little Martha, who had wandered down the beach collecting shells. A strange, bearded man walked up to her in the surf. He smiled and said, "Hi, little girl," and patted her head. Little Martha squealed and ran from him out into the water. A big wave rolled her underwater, and she dropped her bucket. She came up sputtering, her eyes stinging from the sudden dose of salt, her bathing suit all sandy. She crawled out of the surf, whimpering, and a bunch of big kids ran by her. One of them bounced a beach ball off her head and hooted.

Little Martha forgot all about her pail and shells and ran back to the blanket. She fell into her mother's arms and held her in a desperate grip. "Mommy!" she screamed, "I need you!"

"What's wrong? What happened?"

"I just need you, Mommy! I just do!"

Dan, slightly annoyed, walked back to the car to fetch Irene's handbag with its pouch of Kleenex. Tommy went along, too.

"Oh, Christ almighty!" Dan said. The head of the parking meter had been knocked clean off, leaving only the pole. The blue paint of the car's hood was marred by a long gash, where the head of the meter had skated across it. "For crying out loud—look at that damage." He turned on his son. "Let this be a lesson to you, Tommy. This world is full of creeps."

Tommy looked at the headless parking-meter pole and then at the scarred hood and then at his father's red face.

"Freaking maniacs," Dan said, shaking his head, as he and Tommy walked back to the beach with the handbag. "No matter where you go, you can't get away from the maniacs."

Can't get away from the maniacs, Tommy thought.

On the beach, Irene was feeling scared and relieved. Her little girl had wandered off, and all sorts of terrible things might have happened to her. What if she had been caught in the undertow and carried out to sea? Or injured in one of those ways only children can be injured in a place as complex and full of danger as a public beach?

Irene shuddered and held her girl close. In between whimpers, little Martha managed to say, "A man scared me, Mommy."

Irene imagined the worst, some serial pedophile at large in the camouflage of beachwear, striped umbrellas, and volleyball games. Was no place safe anymore? It had been a mistake to come here today, she was sure. They were lucky it had not been worse.

"Everything will be all right," she cooed. She scanned the faces of the people nearby, trying to read their souls. The harder she looked, the blacker they became. It suddenly dawned on her that behind any one of those smiling, placid faces might lurk a beast that prowled on the dark side of human conscience, unrestrained, unaccountable. To anything.

She held her baby close.

By the time Dan and Tommy returned, the food was gone. Little Martha was still whimpering, and the sun was covered by clouds. The wind picked up and flung sand against their bare legs and arms and into their faces. Tommy couldn't even see to read. Plenty of people were leaving the beach, lugging armchairs and towels.

"Some day this turned out to be," Dan said, handing over the tissue and starting to tell Irene about the parking meter.

"I don't want to hear it," she said. "I think we should just go home."

So they lugged all their stuff back to the car, which wouldn't start right away because Dan kept flooding the carburetor.

"Give it room to breathe," Irene said, trying to conceal her impatience. She just couldn't depend on Dan in a crisis.

"Cars don't breathe. What do you know about cars?"

"The man at the gas station always says it has to breathe."

Dan thought about the deserted gas station and flooded the carburetor again. His family sweltered in the heat. Little Martha's bathing suit itched from sand and salt, and she fussed. At last the engine turned over. "Hey, what happened to the hood?" Irene asked. She had been too busy hustling the kids into the car before to notice the hideous scratch.

"Some maniac," Dan said, "knocked the freaking parking meter all to hell."

"Watch your language."

Unintentionally, as he pulled out too fast, he spun a tire and sprayed gravel.

"Watch it," Irene said.

Dan drove back over the causeway while Tommy read the hair-raising finish of his mystery. The sinister tunnel-stalker turned out to be an ally against the real enemy, who came from above. Naturally Frank saved Joe at the last possible second, the treasure was recovered, and the boys' father, himself a professional detective, had words of praise and admiration for the way the boys had handled things. That was some family, that Hardy bunch. Tommy imagined himself sitting around the supper table with them, trading anecdotes about bewildering cases, close calls, modern sleuthing techniques, suspicious characters in the neighborhood.

Little Martha fell into a child's deep sleep. The radio played pop songs.

It was already dusky on the highway, and Dan didn't look forward to driving after dark. He looked around at his family as if they were strangers. Who had made them? How had they all got here, in his car? Dan took a shortcut, and the traffic eased.

"Are you sure this is the right way?" Irene asked.

"You don't trust me much, do you."

The jingly music on the radio quit and a chipper voice came on reading the news headlines. Tommy was dozing, and the news infiltrated his dreams. There was indeed a maniac on the loose. He had killed an entire family over by Glassboro, decapitated them one by one. He was easily recognizable by a long, livid scar across his forehead, just below the hairline.

Tommy was dreaming that they were all parking meters, lined up neatly along the street where they lived. The man with the muddy boots tromped along with a heavy spade and stopped at each one. Then he swung the big spade *thwack*! and another head was lopped off. The heads spun through the air like softballs and thudded onto the pavement. Tommy was next.

The light ahead turned red. Dan braked the car and listened to the engine idle. Because he had left the shift in "drive," the idle was rough, and he needed a firm foot on the brake to keep the car from edging forward into the intersection.

The light stayed red.

"What's wrong with the light?"Tommy said, suddenly awake, draping his arms over the back of the front seat.

"Nothing. It's just a light."

A minute passed, then another. The light stayed red.

"I guess it doesn't want us to go any farther," Dan joked.

"It's been red too long," Irene said. "Just go."

"The light's red, Irene."

"Just go! What's the matter with you? Are we going to sit here all night? My God, show some initiative."

In the rearview mirror, Dan saw a car pull up on them fast, dazzling him with its high beams. It was so close behind them Dan could hear the powerful rev of its engine.

"Are we just going to sit here?" Irene said. Her voice was shrill and her neat ponytail was coming undone. "Are we just not going anywhere, is that it?"

"Come on, Dad! Let's get out of here!"Tommy said.

Little Martha started crying.

Irene was nearly hysterical. "Let me drive, I'll get us out of here! Good Lord, it's just a red light!"

"Calm down, calm down. Maybe it's stuck."The headlights in the rearview mirror made him squint, and the throbbing engine seemed closer, more threatening. He wanted to tell the other driver to cool it, but he dared not step out of the car.

"You're stuck!" Irene said.

"I can't just run a red light—"

"Go, Dan! Go! For once in your life show a little goddammed backbone!" Irene grabbed the wheel and thrust a foot toward the accelerator. She crimped Dan hard on the instep, and he yelped in pain. Reflexively, Dan thrust Irene back to her side of the car, too late to stop the car from shooting forward into the intersection. Irene's head bounced off the window.

The car behind followed them through the intersection and, as Dan finally regained control of his automobile, he heard the siren and saw the flashing Mars lights. He gave up. He stopped on the shoulder, turned off the ignition, and sat slumped over the wheel, his hands in plain sight at the nine and six o'clock positions. Irene's forehead was bleeding.

The officer shot his giant flashlight into the car. "Hey, what's going on here?"

Irene stepped out of the car and stumbled around to where the officer stood.

"Are you all right, ma'am? You're bleeding—"

"You're damned right I'm bleeding!" She showed off the gash on her head.

Little Martha was squalling like a cat, and Tommy sat rigid and breathing fast.

"Officer, I can explain—"

"Out of the car. Slowly."

Dan slunk out and put his hands behind his back. The slap of the handcuffs was cold and final.

Tommy watched the big cop. In the headlights he watched his boots and the black bulk of his gun, all wrapped up in its black holster. He listened to the boots scrape along the gravel of the shoulder. From the mean look on the cop's face, Tommy feared, at any moment, that he might draw his pistol and shoot all of them just for running a red light.

His mother and father talked, loudly at first, and then more reasonably. His father hobbled around on his sore foot, hands pinned behind him. Tommy slumped low against the door so only his eyes were above the rim. No other cars passed. The boots scraped every time the trooper shifted his weight. The black gun bobbed on his hip. Sometimes he leaned his hand against it casually, knuckles folded, and Tommy held his breath.

After a lot more talking, they had it all straightened out. The ticket for running the red light was sixty-eight dollars. The trooper unlocked the handcuffs. Irene had calmed down. Seated beside Dan once again in the front seat, she dabbed his handkerchief to her head and said, "Don't worry about it, Dan. But you should, you know, take charge more often."

But Dan did worry. Here he was riding along with this family that had somehow come to be his, and it was his hopeless duty to protect them against threats he could not even imagine. He thought of that poor family over in Glassboro. How did one take charge of a homicidal maniac?

Dan's wrists still itched where the handcuffs had cut him. They rode on in a difficult silence.

As they turned the corner onto their street, Dan noticed, in the sweep of headlights across the McPhersons' yard, half a dozen neat mounds of leaves and debris. It must have taken hours of raking.

Then he saw similar clumps on his own lawn, and his wrists itched worse than ever.

"For crying out loud," he said. He swung the car into the driveway and punched off the headlights. Before he could turn off the ignition, he noticed the cellar light was on.

"Tommy—did you leave a light on in the cellar?"

"No, not me," Tommy said. But, really, he wasn't sure.

Dan couldn't bring himself to get out of the car. They were home, but what was that light doing on? He rubbed his wrists.

"What are we going to do, Dan?" Irene said—softly, more softly than she had spoken all day. Little Martha tucked her head onto Tommy's lap, right on top of his book, and sucked her thumb hard. Tommy could feel his shirt getting wet from her slobber and tears. Tommy locked his door and wished to hell he was Joe Hardy. He wished they hadn't stopped at that stupid, deserted gas station or had their stupid parking meter smashed or taken a stupid shortcut that got them all into trouble with that stupid cop.

He listened for the scrape of boots on gravel and watched the lighted cellar window at the far end of the house. Above it was the living room, with two windows. To the right was a bathroom window, a hallway window, a dining room with two windows, the pantry window, then the kitchen with two windows. Off the kitchen was a wooden stoop, and the driveway ran right past that into the wooden garage directly ahead.

The other two cellar windows were dark—how could that be? Tommy tried remembering what might be piled in front of each to block the light, and couldn't. An upended mattress? Boxes stacked too high? Were they painted over? No, they were not painted over. He wished his arm were long enough to reach over little Martha and across the broad seat and lock the other door.

"What are we going to do?" Irene said again. She was slipping away. She was not up to this. She felt a sudden surge of remorse for what she had done to Dan. Her own wrists itched from the handcuffs. She had been foolish to imagine that a highway patrolman would make her safe, from anything. She could not think of what to say to Dan now.

She almost remembered why she had married him, almost wanted to commit her future again into his keeping.

Dan stared at the cellar window and then up at all the other dark windows. He stared at the shadowy lumps on the lawn. His hands still gripped the wheel. He felt all of his fragile bones and the lack of real power in his flimsy muscles. He sat quietly, hardly daring to breathe, in his own car, in his own driveway, surrounded by his own family, afraid to go into his own house.

They sat, all of them, prepared to wait all night for the sun to come up over the back of the house, for the one lighted cellar window to go invisible with the dawn.

II.

AND SO THEY MIGHT have, but this was not a day to end with patience. This was a day shot through with the uncanny, a day when all bets were off, when the invisible protective force field that keeps horror out of routine lives was not operating, and ordinary people like the Johnsons were visited by the dangerous intelligence of the world.

So when he saw the light in the cellar window, he knew what he had to do. He pulled a tire iron out from under the seat.

"Lock the door behind me," he told Irene. He slipped the house key off the key ring still in the ignition and left the car running. "Keep the headlights out so you don't give me away and honk the horn if you see anything suspicious. Tommy, keep your eyes peeled."

Tommy nodded, then climbed out from under little Martha and into the front seat.

Dan took a deep breath and headed up the driveway, patting his left palm with the hot iron.

In the ambient street light that dimly reached through the twisted branches of the old elm trees in the front yard, Irene and Tommy could see him turn the key in the kitchen door and go in. Immediately, the kitchen windows lit up. Some of the light spilled out onto the stoop.

On the kitchen stoop, leaning against the house, stood a rake.

At the far end of the house, right above the lighted cellar window, the living room windows suddenly lit up, too. Irene could see Dan through a kitchen window, so it could not have been Dan who turned on the living room light. She honked the horn. Dan waved. Then he was gone from the kitchen window.

Next the pantry light went on, and with it the light in the bathroom adjacent to the living room. Two sets of lights, converging on each other from opposite ends of the house. Irene gasped and leaned on the horn, drawing no reaction from the house. Tommy pounded the dashboard with his fist, hurting his hand. Little Martha cried and cried.

Irene watched the hall window next to the bathroom light up. Whoever it was, he was moving toward Dan. She thought she saw a hunched shadow, but she couldn't be sure. Tommy pounded harder on the dash. Irene blasted the horn and held it.

The dining room windows were still dark. Would Dan go in there?

Would the other? Only those two dark windows remained between them. The car was in neutral gear, idling high because Irene's foot was pressed firmly onto the accelerator. This she didn't even realize.

She waited and waited, and Tommy pounded, and little Martha cried, and the engine raced. "Come on, Dan!" she said out loud, "Come on!"

When at last the dining room windows were flooded with light, she glimpsed a quick Dan-shaped shadow gliding past the pantry window, past the kitchen windows, out onto the stoop.

What was he looking at?

Behind him appeared another man, raising a baseball bat.

The Dan-shaped shadow moved into the driveway and looked off toward the McPhersons', holding something black in his hand, as the other raised the bat.

Irene did not hesitate. She jammed the gearshift into "drive" and the car shot forward. She aimed for the man holding the baseball bat next to the kitchen stoop.

She felt the body bump under the chassis. The bat starred the windshield and rattled off. Then the night went deadly still. The radiator steamed and ticked. It was some moments before Irene could make herself get out of the car, now tilted on top of the wooden stoop.

When she opened her door and stepped out, she saw a hand and arm sticking out from under the car. She saw a black felt hat lying on the ground. He had to be dead.

She pulled out the headlight knob. She walked around the front of the car. Tommy had wet his pants. He climbed out and stood next to his mother. She looked at the ground by the passenger door and screamed, hoarsely: the body lay hidden in the ragged black shadow of elm branches, but it was not wearing muddy boots.

"Lord have mercy!" Irene said. Tommy was too scared even to scream.

Little Martha at last climbed out of the car and sat down next to the body on the driver's side. She picked up a white deck shoe that had been knocked off at impact. "Daddy?" she said, and jammed her thumb firmly into her mouth. She rocked back and forth in her sundress.

Tommy heard the rasp of boots and looked over at the kitchen door. Backlit by the friendly glow of the overhead fixture in the kitchen was a smiling man Tommy had never seen before in his life.

"Welcome home," the man said in a colorless voice. "How was the beach?"

When he brushed the black hair off his forehead, Tommy saw the long, thick scar.

III.

I'VE TOLD THIS STORY before, and I'll tell it again, because part of me is Dan, frozen with indecision, and a bigger part of me is Tommy, imagination burrowed deep into the certain comfort of the Hardy Boys. And each time I tell it, it comes a little more true, so that what you hear, along with the story, is always the story of the last telling of the story, approaching the true ending of the Johnson family.

Somewhere between the slasher-movie climax of slaughtered innocents confounded by a brilliant maniac and the artful vision of sunrise bleaching away the menace lies the truth, what really happened when the Johnson family arrived home.

It matters what happened.

They did sit in the car, in the driveway, too frightened to go into their own house. That much I'm sure of. Little Martha was crying like her heart would break.

Tommy wanted action from somebody older, stronger, more confident, and a memory that would not betray him—had he really left the light on in the cellar?

I don't know what Irene said to Dan. At this moment in the story, in the eternal present tense of stories, I am outside the car looking in. The windows are wound up tight. If they speak at all, it is in whispers, guarded murmurs, mouth close to ear.

I gave them a bad time at the beach. I did it on purpose. I detoured them into an unattended gas station, vandalized their parking meter, stopped them at a red light that wouldn't turn green, even set the cops on them.

Then I left a light on in their cellar and let a creepy stranger hang around their empty house all day raking leaves into dead piles.

But they did the rest. If there was any maniac, they invented him.

At the end I stand outside their car, invisible in the moon shadows of the great crooked elms on the front lawn, and watch. What I see is this: Irene takes Dan's hand. It's not a romantic gesture, not the way it looks from out here. It's not even a gesture of forgiveness, or hope, or love. But it is a gesture of need, and there is loyalty in that. She sits in the car, holding his hand. That's the way it looks from out here. They could indeed be at a drive-in movie, except for the bawling kid in the backseat.

They're not in love, not anymore—if they ever were. If they ever will be again, if that is even possible.

In a single moment, their whole lives have come down to this: two frightened people, sitting in a car. They've been together for years. Without the home they have made, they'd be as lost and hopeless as deer on a highway. They've made children together, but that was a long time ago.

Just lately, just this morning in fact, they tried to do the simplest thing a family could do, go to the beach, and they failed. They know it. They aren't happy about it. It scares them. They don't know where to go from here, and they're both dead sure that whatever move they make, right now, at this moment, will be the wrong one.

Once they leave the car, all bets are off. There are many things they may never do again.

And the children's whole lives stretch before them in a sudden parody of epiphany. When he gets out of that car, Tommy will be done with the Hardy Boys forever. They can't help him now. He needs something else, something more—and he knows it. He wishes he didn't know it.

In a dozen years Little Martha will be telling this story to a college roommate as they sit up late and sip golden Chablis and watch an older moon rise outside their high window. She'll sit cross-legged on her dormitory bed and pull the fresh coverlet over her bare legs. Reciting the story of her parents sitting in that old car will be for her like telling a ghost story.

She will never get over it.

She will go through life certain that her future changed at that hour, that moment, when her parents sat in front of a house with one lighted cellar window—but she will never understand exactly why, or how. She will stare at that window all her life, wondering.

Someday she will have a child of her own and, when she and her husband go out to the movies, she will leave lights on in every room of the house. But she will never once return home without knowing that little thrill in her stomach as she rounds the last corner onto her street, and watches for the lighted windows of her own house. And no matter how many lights she has left on, no matter whether she enters alone or in company, she will always enter her own home with a fluttering heart.

So, sitting in the driveway, the engine idling, Irene holds Dan's hand. It is not the signature of a happy ending. But she holds his hand anyway. She knows, as he knows, that one of them will have to get out of the car first and go to the kitchen door. She knows, as he knows, that it will be Dan. And that once he walks away into the shadows, approaches the door and turns the key in the lock, everything may be different.

So they wait just a little longer. She holds his hand and will not let it go. Dan would not want her to. They went away on a journey. They came back. Meanwhile, a stranger has come into their lives. And this is their homecoming, and everything is different now.

"Who turned on the light?" she says.

"I don't know," Dan says.

"And who was that strange man this morning?"

Dan says, "We may never know."

"You're going inside, aren't you," Irene says.

"I have to," Dan says. "You know that."

"Not yet," she says, squeezing his hand tighter, "not yet."

Davey Terwilliger

Mrs. Terwilliger lay dying in her bedroom that summer, and we played baseball every day with her sons. Davey was going on twelve, a small, wiry, tow-headed boy. His little brother Natty tagged along everywhere, a snot-nosed eight-year-old with permanently mussed dark hair and a slouchy walk, as if he were afraid to stand up straight, that maybe somebody might knock him down. He was lousy at baseball, but we always let him play anyway because of Davey.

Davey was usually captain of one team or another. He played shortstop and pitched sometimes and had a tight, hard swing.

He had no choice but to bring Natty along, since he couldn't just leave him at home. He packed Natty's lunch and bought him sodas from the gas station with his paper-route money, and whenever Natty scraped his knee or stubbed his toe, Davey would fish a Band-Aid out of his dungarees pocket and gently smooth it onto the wound and say, "Don't cry, little brother. I got you covered." His father was some kind of professor and kept erratic hours. I think Davey must have cooked all their meals, any meals that were cooked, that is.

Their mother had been no help to either boy in a long time—though I recall her in summers past leaning on the chain link fence that separated our houses and chatting with my mother as she hung wash on the line. Then she started dying. It was a small subdivision, a neighborhood where people scolded each other's children and borrowed tools and waved at each other on the street. And talked about Mrs. Terwilliger dying mysteriously in her bedroom.

I remember it was a Thursday when it happened, because that was the day we always got supplements to stuff into the newspapers we delivered from canvas sacks slung across one shoulder. We hated supplements—all that extra weight to carry. I had finished my route, and we were eating supper when Mr. Polk, from up the street, came to the door. He spoke in low tones to my father. I heard him say, "Doctor's there," and "Poor woman won't last the night," and there was more that I didn't hear. My father turned to my mother and said, tiredly, "I have to help find him," and the two men went out into the cloudy bright twilight.

"What's wrong?" I asked my mother.

"Mister Terwilliger has gone off again."

The men of the neighborhood were hunting him like a posse. He did this from time to time—went off. Sometimes they found him in the woods without his clothes, or prancing along Baltimore Road in his bathrobe and slippers. The men hunted a long time, and it was after dark when they shined a flashlight in his eyes as he cowered in the Fitches' cellarway, sobbing his eyes out.

When they got him home, Davey and little Natty were gone. I knew where to find them. I pedaled through the woods path to the baseball diamond behind the school, and I remember how the moon lit up the path like a flood lamp. First, I heard Natty bawling like a goat. He was sitting on the visitors bench wailing and snotting, hugging his knees to his chest, rocking. Davey stood backwards in the batter's box. He flipped a ball up and then swung the bat and whacked the ball into the backstop. He did this over and over. Each time, the bat made a dull crack, and the ball *zinged* into the chain-link, and he muttered something as he retrieved the ball. I got closer, so close he almost hit me with the bat, and I felt it whiff past my cheek. He didn't even know I was there. His eyes were furious, without tears. His arms and neck and face were coated in sweat and dust. He batted the ball into the mesh and stomped toward it, muttering, "When do I get to, when do I get to, when do I?"

The Man Who Fell Out of the Sky

His wife, Patricia, asked me to do it. She called me in San Diego late in the afternoon of a rainy Sunday, when it was already night in the Midwest. "Connor?" she said, and then paused for a long time. "Rick's dead." The clear silence of the long-distance line whined in my ear. "You're his best friend," she said softly, as if she were afraid I'd hang up on her. "I didn't know who else to call."

"Me," I told her. "I was the right one to call."

I have always been the one trusted to make such calls, because they know I can tell the bad news straight out. When my kid brother Jimmy got killed in a car wreck three years back, my mother asked me to call the others. Judy asked me the same favor when Greta, her college roommate, died of cancer last spring.

It took a minute to catch my breath, but I wasn't feeling anything yet, just a hollow light-headedness, as I listened to my voice stupidly trying to say something that would help.

After Patricia hung up, I sat in the den with my Rolodex, poured out a slug of Scotch and let it burn my tongue a while, tried to figure out who ought to be told in what order. Judy first—I knew that much. Judy and Rick had known each other forever, since even before I met him in college. It had happened outside Chicago, almost two hours ago. It would be late in Washington, D.C., where Judy lived. I punched in her number and waited three, four rings, until she picked up.

"Hey, Connor! Just got done eating a late supper. Where are you—in town?"

"Judy, I've got to tell you something. Rick is dead." That's the best way to tell these things—straight out, matter-of-fact, fast, get it over with. I listened, the telephone line clear as a needle of ice strung across the continent, and imagined her leaning against the shining white counter in her townhouse kitchen, the clean spare kitchen of a woman who lived alone and always would. "Judy?"

Then I heard her breathing, a little sob. "I'm here, Connor."

"I'm sorry to be the one."

"I'm glad it was you. Jesus. Oh, Jesus."

"Yeah, I know. I know."

"How did it, when did he—?"

"Couple of hours ago." I told her what I knew: Rick was flying a rented Cessna, just out for a ride. They were in the air about ten minutes. Then the plane just fell out of the sky. There was a witness. "Nobody knows what went wrong." It's the first thing people always ask, what happened? How come? Like if there's a good answer to that, they can handle it. It will make sense.

"They?"

"Rick and another guy, a pilot friend. Nobody we know."

"Rick was the one flying?"

"They don't know. Could have been. Plane had dual controls."

I was surprised at how easily I told it. I could just see the yellow plane cutting across the sunset, the raddled light glancing off its flat, stubby wings, then spinning out of the sky into a cornfield. Patricia had said it was a yellow plane with silver wings. There was no fire. The airplane slammed into the ground and burst apart. Rick was thirty-six, my age. He had two little girls. We have a son—Rick was his godfather. Away at summer camp.

"Who have you called so far?" Judy asked.

"Just you, sweetie. Had to tell you first."

"Thanks," she whispered. "You always know what to do."

But all I know is that there is a secret order to grief, that knowledge of death is precious and not to be shared lightly. When I hung up, my hand was shaking. I took another shot and went down my list. One call, one shot. Not the kind of drinking I was used to, not the kind that makes you drunk or softens the hard edges, but I had to maintain my composure to get through this.

Martin in Las Vegas. Ty in Rhode Island. Megan and Jerry in Delaware. Janet, who was up in LA now. All of us just old friends from somewhere—college, jobs, places where we'd lived together. Martin his old college roommate, Ty his neighbor from Providence, Megan and Jerry who had once taught with him at a college in Florida, Janet who had dated Rick's little brother in the Marines before he got killed in Beirut—another set of calls I'd made. Their claims all sorted themselves out according to a logic I can't really explain. But there was a right order.

Patricia couldn't call any of them—she had always been outside the circle, just "Rick's wife." Somebody'd throw a party and say, be sure to invite Rick and his wife. Not her name.

Each call went about the same way. They all wanted to know exactly how it happened, and did he live after the crash, and who was the other guy. And who else had I called? I was on the phone for about three hours.

I'm an accountant– what do I know about flying? But I know things have to add up. "He never knew what hit him," I assured all of them, but that had to be a lie. I kept imagining Rick fighting the joystick for all those seconds while the plane plummeted, and the world came up to meet him square in the face. For however long it took to fall from three thousand feet to zero—a minute? Minute and a half? He knew he was going to die.

But in my imagination, I couldn't hear him scream in panic. All I could hear was the other guy in the cockpit telling Rick to quit fucking around. They were up there screwing around, doing tricks—I was sure of it—and things got out of control. Maybe the other guy froze up, wouldn't let loose of the stick. Maybe he had a heart attack. Maybe the other guy put them into a steep dive without enough altitude to pull out. Maybe he was a suicide case. But I was pretty sure it had been Rick's fault—he always pushed it. Those last moments, that long fall—I kept going over it in my head, the way you stick your tongue into the socket of a missing tooth just to make it hurt.

I sat in the den and stared out the window until it got light. Then I perked a pot of coffee and tried to gather myself. I took a long, steamy shower. There was one call I had not made, to my wife Emily. She was flying in from Paris with her sister, and there was no way to reach her. They'd been in transit since noon yesterday, when she'd called from Charles de Gaulle to say that all was well.

Emily came through customs right on time, she and her sister Suzie lugging fancy parcels and carry-ons. I grabbed some of the bags and wrapped a hug around them both. "Welcome home," I said. I must have looked awful—Emily kissed me on the ear and whispered, "Tell me what's wrong."

In the car, I had trouble with the sun. I'd forgotten my sunglasses. "I've already made reservations," I told her.

"Anybody but Rick," Emily whispered. Rick had introduced us, when we lived in Chicago. He had met Emily during jury duty and invited her to a party he was throwing for Ty's birthday. Losing him was like losing our courtship. He was in our wedding album.

"Never had any sense," I said to the windshield.

Emily said, "Shh."

RICK HAD BEEN DEAN of students at a little college up on the North Shore, and, next day when we got in, the college would hold a memorial service for him. That evening there was to be a wake and the following day the funeral.

At the airport Hilton, I put on my charcoal suit and we drove up to the college, which looked like the set for a sentimental Bing Crosby movie. The whole student body had crammed into the stone chapel and two of the students gave little speeches about what a good guy Rick was, what a terrific math teacher. And he *was* a good guy—the sort who would lend his car to a stranger and open his wallet for any worthy cause. He coached Little League soccer and served with the United Way. The kind of guy that keeps a community in business.

Then a third student went to the podium and read a sappy poem, and it got everybody crying. I always hate that sort of thing. We all felt bad enough—there was no reason to ramp it up with phony clichés. We spotted Patricia afterward and walked under big elm trees toward the rental car. It hit me all of a sudden—she was a widow now.

"Thanks for coming all this way," she said. Her pupils were dilated—I guess they had given her something. Her words came slow and thick. "I didn't know if you would really come."

"Of course, what did you think?" I touched her arm like I was patting a piece of wood. "If you need any help," I said, "going over the papers."

"Papers," she said dreamily. "I guess there are papers somewhere." She walked looking straight ahead, and some relatives trailed her with her two little girls, who were dressed in white crinoline like dolls, their blonde hair combed out long. They held hands. For the next few days Patricia, now Rick's widow, would enjoy a kind of privileged status, with everybody doing for her and trying to cushion her from all the routine stuff of the world and the non-routine stuff that comes with an intimate death. But I was already thinking how it would be for her in a couple of weeks, a couple of months, next year maybe, when everybody else went back to their own business, and she was alone, waking up to it first thing every morning and going to bed with it last thing every night.

"Anything we can do," I said. I was looking around for Judy, for Megan and Jerry, Martin, Ty, and Janet.

"Judy's plane should be landing in about an hour," Patricia said. "If you could go out there."

"Right, leave it to me." I had to get away from her and the lovely, cozy campus and just try to get through this thing.

"The college is going to keep up the health insurance," Patricia said, "for another whole year." Her voice sounded mechanical, like she was lost somewhere, and somebody else was doing the talking. I wanted to tell her that a year is no time at all in this life, that she would be floundering in debt before she knew it, but at that moment it seemed impossible that anything could be predicted for a whole year in advance. Time had been stretching out and contracting ever since I got the news.

JUDY WAS ALREADY AT the baggage carousel by the time we got to O'Hare. She was wearing a black suit with a gray, silk chemise and heels. Her shining black hair was braided French-style. She hugged me and then hugged Emily, and I carried her bag out to the car. When we got back to the hotel she ordered up ice and vodka, "a nice clean drink," she said, and we all sat in our good clothes in the air conditioning and watched out the picture window as the planes glided into O'Hare.

"You okay?" I asked Judy.

"I cried on the plane. Yeah, I'm okay."

Emily said, "I can't imagine what Patricia's going to do now."

Judy stared out the window, where a bulgy 747 was lifting into the air, which at that moment seemed completely impossible.

Emily said, "The kids. What does she tell the kids?"

I couldn't get it out of my head: those last seconds, falling toward the earth. What goes through a man's mind? "Never had any sense," I said. "The hell did he think he was doing?"

"I thought he'd given up flying," Judy said. "That's what he told me." Judy and Rick had once been involved—years before Patricia. A sexy friendship, Rick called it. Just slipped back and forth over the line, always half in love and half just fucking around. Nobody ever mentioned it to Patricia.

Rick told me years after the fact, the only time he ever took me flying. "Anything I tell you up here in the wild blue is strictly between us, partner," he said from behind his bottle-green aviator's glasses. He had the lean face of a flyer, the square chin, the thinning, black hair cut military short.

Hanging with him in the clear sky over lake Michigan, I had felt privy to all his secrets. "Ask me anything up here," he'd said, but I didn't have to. I never told anybody else, but I think they all guessed. Years after Rick married Patricia, everybody would ask Judy what was going on with Rick, and she always seemed to know.

"He was always screwing around," I said. "Remember at our wedding?" Rick had dived off a second story balcony into the pool at a hotel just like this one. Still wearing his tux.

Emily said, "That was nothing compared to the cherry bomb he planted in our toilet. In the honeymoon suite."

"He never knew when to quit," Judy agreed and laughed. As I watched her stare out the window and sip vodka from a water glass, it hit me. The hard way she was drinking, the extra carelessness in her voice: their affair had never ended. Not in her mind. All this time, it had gone on—true honest love, thoughtless, reckless. It was in the tilt of her head, the sure way her hand gripped the glass and rattled the ice cubes, the sense that she felt entitled and cheated. All this grief was hers.

Emily was watching, too. She said, "Where are the others? Aren't they coming?"

"Half an hour after you hung up, the calls started," Judy said and refilled her glass. "Ty has to go to New York on business. Megan and Jerry have houseguests. Janet couldn't afford the fare. Martin just said he was tied up." There was no surprise in her voice, just dismissal.

"Doesn't matter," I said. "Rick wouldn't want everybody gawking at him."

Emily said, "For some things, you make time."

I said, "It's not always that simple." People have their lives, and they spin out in complicated orbits.

"I miss them," Judy said. "They should have come. I mean, I didn't want to come, either."

"Drink up," I said, "then let's have some supper before we go."

"I can't eat anything," Judy said.

"Me, neither," Emily said.

So we sat and watched the planes drift out of the sky, and then I went upstairs to our room with Emily to let her cry in private.

LATER WE WENT TO the mortuary and viewed the body, which resembled Rick, but the hair was combed wrong and the necktie had a dimple below the knot, which is not how a man ties his own tie. Seeing his body was like telling a lie and then finding out it wasn't a lie after all. I had been the one to spread the news, but until that moment I had not believed it in my stomach.

I had not expected an open casket—not for a plane crash. He didn't even look hurt. There wasn't a mark on his face.

The other thing was—I don't know why—I had expected there would be two caskets, Rick's and the other guy's, whoever he was. For some reason, I had expected that since the two of them had died together inside that little cockpit, they'd naturally be buried together. It seemed wrong to separate them. When I asked, nobody knew anything about the other guy. Patricia had never met him. She didn't even remember his name.

THE FUNERAL THE NEXT day was short and proper, crowded with students and relatives and friends of Patricia's. Afterward, there was a little reception at the house. We had coffee and stood around in our best clothes without him.

"Did I tell you?" Patricia said. "The college is going to keep up the health insurance?" and we nodded. She stood there like she was waiting for somebody to say something that would make time start up again for her. Emily sipped her coffee. Judy tipped a flask of vodka into her cup and offered some to me, but I declined. She wasn't being very discreet, but I didn't feel I had any right to say so. Patricia wasn't fazed. She gripped Judy's arm. "Look—you have to help me here."

Judy stared at her blankly but did not pull away.

"What I mean, this is all new. We have the health plan, sure. But. There's nothing to go by. You see? There's nothing."

"Of course," Judy said, a little slurry, but I don't think she understood at all. The two women stood together in a tableau, the shy housewife and the chic lawyer, the one asking and the other not comprehending what was being asked of her.

Patricia kept talking. "There's nobody, there's—to tell me what I should do now. If the kids get sick, I mean we have insurance, but. The college. I never thought this would happen. We never talked about it. What are the rules? I mean, there have to be some steps to follow—"

I took Patricia's hand and loosened it from Judy's arm. "Patricia," I said. "Shh. Take it easy."

Judy said, with great tenderness, "You loved him. You make up the rest."

Patricia nodded, grateful I think, and composed herself with a strength I did not suppose she had. For that moment, she looked like the proud, captivating girl Rick had fallen in love with all those years ago.

Then Patricia's mother and aunt came along and gentled her between them to a bedroom somewhere to give her what she needed, or what they thought she needed—soft voices in her ear and hands to hold and the start of the slow countdown of the seconds and hours of the rest of her life.

When she had gone, Judy said, "She'll be married again within the year. Some car salesman or whatever."

"Come on, Judy," I said. "Don't be that way. It's a strain. God knows—"

"She has a right to certain things," Emily said.

Judy finished her spiked coffee, then filled the cup to the brim from her flask. She took a long gulp. "So do I."

"Don't get started," I said. "Not here. Not now."

"What am I saving it for?"

There was an emptiness in the air, like the whole world had gone quiet, like all the important stuff in our lives was happening somewhere else.

In our dark sunglasses we sat by the pool with Judy, the only one drinking, and we talked quietly of the ones who were not there— Martin in Las Vegas, Ty in Rhode Island, Megan and Jerry in Delaware. Janet in LA. "They're all the people in my life," Judy said. And what she didn't say was that Rick had been the center, all the rest of us just spokes on the wheel. After this, it was unlikely any of us would ever see each other again, unless by accident.

"They're good people," I said. "The best." At that instant, the world seemed a fragile crust, eggshell-thin, and if I wasn't careful I might break through and keep falling. I did not dare move, or talk too loud.

"But where are they all? Why am I spending my life with all those other people instead?"

"What do you want me to say?"

"No, I mean it," Judy insisted. "The people I see every day? The guys I work with, the people next door, I don't give a shit about them. Who are they? They're not mine."

"That's just how it is," I said. "Jobs, families, stuff."

"Where is everybody? Where the hell?"

"Judy—"

"It's like, like I spend my life in one place with a crowd of people I don't even know, and all *my* people are someplace else. *My* people are flung to the fucking four winds."

A couple of teenagers splashed around in the pool, but they were just props, like the blue-striped umbrellas over the tables or the kid in the red jacket setting up a bar under the ramada. The world swarmed with people who didn't matter.

I thought about when the time would come to bury me, who would be standing next to my wife telling her what comes next. Who would get on a plane and go through all this just to make it come true. I couldn't imagine anything beyond the uneven breeze flapping the blue umbrellas and the shriek of planes landing and taking off across the board fence. In the sunlight, I finally cried until my throat burned.

WE FLEW HOME THAT night. We always seemed to be on planes, skimming along at the edge of outer space, disconnected from the natural flux and rhythm of the ground. Judy was on another plane flying fast in the opposite direction, already a whole time zone removed. For once, Emily and I were traveling together. I sat by the window, and Emily slept with her head on my shoulder, and the warm weight of her there was my heart, soaring along into the future at six hundred miles per hour through the starry blackness of thirty thousand feet.

While down below, in the darkness between cities, the telephone lines were humming with bad news, people scattered across the continent calling each other about the ones who had fallen out of the sky, trying to gather each other up again, one by one, in the right order.

In Dreams Begin

Last night I had the dream again.

I'm sitting in the stands at Yankee Stadium, where I've never been in real life, and on the field a hubbub begins. A grizzled guy who looks like Yogi Berra points at me, and the umpire and the other players all stare. "Me?" I say, like I always say. They're too far away, so I pantomime, pointing to myself, and they pantomime back, waving me down out of the stands. All the other spectators make way for me. The ushers clear a path. I climb down onto the field. Berra throws a heavy arm around my shoulder, says, "We've got a situation here. Nettles is injured. How'd you like to play third base?"

I say, like I say every time, "I didn't bring my glove."

"We'll get you a glove."

"I didn't bring any cleats."

"We'll give you cleats, a cap, the whole uniform. You don't play, we got to forfeit."

So I play nine innings, go three for five at the plate with two singles and a double off the wall in left that drives in a couple of runs, and make all my chances in the field. We win 5-4. As we're walking through the tunnel back to the clubhouse, just a bunch of winners joshing with each other and the crowd noise fading, I wake up—gently rising from the depths of sleep to the surface of a sunny,

Saturday morning in bed beside my wife, Joan, who looks haggard and sunken-eyed, like she hasn't slept a wink.

"Don't tell me," she says.

"Yep," I say. "Three for five at the plate, two RBI's. We won."

"Five to four," she says. "I know. You always win five to four. Which position did you play this time?"

"Third base."

The thing is, I haven't played baseball since Little League, and I was never very good. Haven't watched a major league game in probably fifteen years. But the dream energizes me, makes me feel like a talented kid, leaves me with a kind of afterglow of contentment, almost like sex. I snuggle close to her and stroke her bare arm. "How about you?"

She sits up and smooths her copper hair back from her temples. "I spent the night roaming around a parking garage in Buenos Aires looking for a rental car I couldn't remember the color of because I was late for a speech I was supposed to give on quantum physics—in Portuguese, naturally. Oh, and did I mention I was naked and being chased by big rats and some creepy guy in a trench coat?"

My wife doesn't know anything about physics, but you knew that. And she speaks fluent German, but not a word of Portuguese. I'm not sure they even speak Portuguese in Buenos Aires.

Last week she was lost in a deserted warehouse in Berlin, a maze of wooden crates and pallets stacked to the ceiling, and she had to get to the airport to catch the last plane to London. And she was naked. A few nights before that, she was late for a class she couldn't find to take an exam she hadn't studied for in a subject she had never heard of. At Beijing University. Naked.

She spends her nights that way—chasing something she can never quite grasp, responsible for things she has no control over, missing flights and blowing exams and screwing up speeches, foolish and crying and vulnerable and always in vague danger, wandering in foreign places, lost, late, confused, worried, frustrated, scared, stymied, inadequate, unprepared, baffled, alone, and naked.

She's the executive secretary to the partners of a small engineering firm that for years has mismanaged itself onto the edge of bankruptcy. They've been doing all sorts of sketchy accounting lately, and Joan keeps telling them they're going to get into trouble, and they just smile and make passes at her. It's not an ideal situation. She'd rather be in a bigger city, but she makes decent money—much more than I do painting houses. We need her income. I don't do all that well. Joan doesn't believe a guy with a PhD in philosophy ought to be a housepainter, but I like the work, gives me time to think. She doesn't bring it up any more.

WE FUSS AROUND THE house all Saturday morning, lazy and slack, then roam the outdoor mall downtown for a couple hours in the afternoon. To lift her spirits, I say I'll treat her to Chinese, which is her favorite. So we have a late lunch at a franchise place called Chow Fats, egg rolls and rice beer, and when the fortune cookies arrive I crack mine open immediately. I love the secret promise of fortune cookies, the anticipation of great good things ahead. I feel the same flutter in my stomach as I do when I flip the mailbox open to see what good news awaits me. My wife dreads the arrival of mail, but then she's the one who writes out the checks to pay all the bills.

I unscroll my fortune and read it. "In Dreams Begin."

"That's it?" she says. "What's that supposed to mean?"

"I don't have a clue." But in my mind I'm already gliding effortlessly to the foul line, scooping up a hot grounder, whipping it sidearm across the long hypotenuse of the infield to nail the runner at first by a step, and my teammates all slap their fists into their gloves and say, *way to go.*

"Let's see yours."

She breaks open the cookie and there is no fortune. She gasps and dashes the halves of the cookie onto the table, where they crumble into pieces.

"It's just a fortune cookie," I say, holding her hand. "Don't get so upset."

I flag the waiter and order two new cookies. "These are defective," I explain, and he looks baffled, but in a moment brings us two fresh cookies.

"Pick whichever one you want," I say.

She eenie-meenie-minie-moes and picks up a cookie, cracks it open. Again, no fortune.

My fortune reads, you guessed it: "In Dreams Begin."

"A defective batch," I say. "Somebody's idea of a bad joke at the cookie plant."

Joan says, "Last August, Erin's friend Lydia got a cookie without a fortune, and she got killed in a car crash a week later."

"Oh, come on—you don't believe that."

But she's so upset I take her straight home and brew her a cup of lemon-zinger tea and we sit on the back porch not talking, just watching the light go gray and listening to the birds make a racket, and finally go inside to watch a little TV and then go to bed.

And now I lie awake, resisting sleep, my eyelids heavy, my body tired from the tension of the day. Somehow if I can stay awake until Joan falls asleep, I have this feeling that she'll be all right tonight, that she won't spend the dark hours wandering parking garages on faraway continents being pursued by spectral figures who want to do her harm while she misses her chance at whatever urgent thing she must accomplish.

At last her breathing is regular, and her slim body is still. I move closer to her, inhale her sweet warmth, wanting to touch her curvy hips and the small of her back but wary of waking her, this woman without a fortune.

Before I drift off, I already know how it is going to be. Tonight I am pitching—it is the only position I haven't played. My arm feels loose and good, my body nimble and strong as sleep overtakes me by gentle degrees. Tonight I have it in me to pitch a no-hitter. I feel this with certainty. A perfect game, maybe.

But even though we were meant for each other, no man and woman were ever more perfectly joined, I cannot protect the woman I love in the dark hours, cannot hold onto her when she retreats into her own troubled imagination, into the unconscious weight of the disappointing life I have given her, into the unsettling stuff of her dreams. She is beyond me then, out of reach, as lonely as a person can ever be.

IN MY LAST WILLFUL moment before I float into my seat at Yankee Stadium, I wish hard for her to join me there. To be at my side, happy and safe, both of us in the same dream. I have two tickets tonight, box seats, and, just once, I want her to be exactly where she belongs, right where she's supposed to be, best seat in the house, with a ticket stub in her pocket to prove it, and the soundtrack of her dream to be the roaring cheers of the crowd, not a deadline clock counting down to panic.

And just once, just once, I want her to see me play.

Things We Do When
No One Is Watching

K ids are closer to the past than we are," I said. I'd had been
thinking all week about a kid I used to know, ever since I'd
read that newspaper piece my father sent me.

"It's silly nostalgia," my wife Lilah said. "We get older and the
world becomes more complicated. We look back longingly on our
childhood, like it holds some secret clue about who we are."

"Maybe it does," I said. This was after-dinner conversation.
Mike and Maeve Riley were over, and we were starting on the
second bottle of Beaujolais. We'd moved into the living room by
the fireplace. "Wait, let me have some of that wine," Mike said.
Over his shoulder, the fire was blazing nicely in the hearth. The
whole place looked just like a home ought to look on a winter's
night.

"No, it doesn't," Lilah insisted. "Your childhood is dead and
gone, cheap memories. Grow up." She's a behavioral psychologist
and no Freudian.

"Listen, when I was growing up in Pennsylvania, there was this
kid named Skippy."

"I had a miserable childhood," Mike said, waving his glass. "I
was a runt, always getting picked on."

I could buy that. Even at forty he was the kind of smart-ass guy you just wanted to sock once in a while. Now he owned a fleet of bulldozers that had scraped clear half the county. He and Lilah got along famously.

"We were all nine or ten in those days. Skippy was a real shrimp, and he had something wrong with his legs."

Lilah sighed. "You're going to tell this anyway, aren't you."

"Polio. He was always in and out of Shriners hospital. Never wore shorts—his legs were all scarred. One day he comes home wearing this elaborate brace that straps on like a gun belt around his waist and has all this leather and steel running down his leg. Lots of buckles and straps."

"Lovely," Lilah said.

"For the first couple of days, we all thought it was pretty neat, Skippy, too. You could whack his leg with a stick and break the stick and not even hurt him. We whacked him plenty for a few days and then the novelty wore off."

"This story has a point, I'm sure," Mike said. "Some kind of miraculous ending?" His eyes had lost their clarity and his face was slack.

Maeve was quiet, her bony, little fingers wrapped around the stem of her wineglass. Her nails were chewed something awful. Mike cupped his glass in his palm, the way I imagined he might cup Maeve's small breast during their lovemaking. Except I couldn't quite picture them making love—even though they're both very short and light-framed, and people always comment on how right they look together. I could picture them in separate beds, or watching TV together from opposite ends of the sofa, not talking much.

"Not exactly. We lived in a little subdivision near the woods, and all summer long that's where we played. Troy Wilson's father had made us all wooden machine guns on his jigsaw, and we used to choose up sides and play guns, you know, ambush one another. Throw stickerballs for grenades, that kind of thing."

"Pretty violent stuff," Lilah said. "Explains a lot."

I've never been comfortable with what my wife does—it troubles me to reduce the miracle of living to stimulus-response. But now wasn't the time to get into that argument. "It was good, healthy fun, running around outdoors all day. Except with all that apparatus on his leg, Skippy couldn't run, he sort of hobbled. Kept getting left behind."

Mike swigged down his wine and poured his glass full, then lit up another cigarette. He passed the bottle over to me. It was a cold winter evening, still early but very dark already, and it was cozy to be indoors with old friends, feeling the warm buzz of the wine, knowing it was a Friday night and we could all sleep in tomorrow.

Maeve excused herself to the powder room, and I waited for her to return. Of all of them, I wanted her to hear this story. She came back and settled herself into the chair next to mine, where she could watch the fire. Her eyes looked red.

"Skippy's old man had been killed in an industrial accident—fell off an oil tank and broke his back. His mother remarried right away, man named Dal Wooten. Big man, always had a red face. Shock of coal-black hair."

Maeve's father had died last year, horribly, in a fire—got sozzled on gin and fell asleep smoking in bed in front of the TV. He had abandoned his family when Maeve was a girl.

"What'd this Dal Wooten do for a living?" Mike said.

"Owned a garage, kept junk cars all over the front yard. Old Dal Wooten used to beat that kid silly, for the least little thing. Used to lock Skippy out of the house in the morning and let him back in for supper. His mother was a boozer. She left a peanut butter sandwich on the stoop for him at lunchtime, and he drank water out of the outdoor faucet."

"Jesus," Lilah said.

"Right. We kids used to make fun of him."

"Little snots. Kids don't know nothing at that age. I sure didn't," Mike said. "Lilah, can I have some more wine?" Lilah passed the bottle down to the end of the couch and then fetched another from the rack in the kitchen. She opened it to let it breathe, and we stopped talking. Everybody likes to watch a fresh bottle of wine being opened. Lilah did it with one of those nifty prong things you slide down on either side of the cork and, *pfft*, out it comes.

"Kids are smarter than you think," I said. "They know stuff. You'd be amazed what they know." I teach them history all day long down at the high school.

"How do you talk to them, I'd like to know," Lilah said. "Even the college freshmen we get for research subjects don't have a clue."

"I like the kids." And it's true—they share their confidences with me so easily it's almost embarrassing, because they know I'll never tell.

"I bet it turned him mean," Mike said.

"Not at all. He was the most carefree kid you ever saw. Nothing fazed him. He'd steal penknives from the hardware store and give them to us. He was always stealing stuff, but he had a special thing for blades."

"Juvenile delinquent," Mike said. "Brings back memories."

"Anyhow, Skippy got tired of the brace. He'd come hobbling out of the house in the morning and go to the woods, then unstrap the brace and stash it behind a tree and run off with the rest of us."

"He could run?" Mike said. "I thought he was crippled."

Lilah said, "We don't use that word, Mike."

"That was the funny thing—without that brace, he could really move, sort of scramble around like a crab. Not very graceful, but quick. Didn't seem to hurt him any."

Maeve watched the fire, not me. "Anyhow, we'd mess around up in the woods, go exploring down by the creek, climb the railroad trestle, typical boy-stuff. After supper, we'd meet under the streetlight and get up a game of kick-the-can, or just sit on the curb and tell spooky stories until our parents started hollering for us to come in."

Telling about it now, I was missing those days: The cool nights toward the end of summer you wanted to last forever because in a few weeks you'd be back at your homework. The quick dash into the shadows of a neighbor's yard, around the back of a house, then hollering, legs pumping, as you raced in to kick the can and set everybody free.

"All except Skippy—he wasn't allowed out at night. We stayed away from his yard so the old man wouldn't yell at us. He was always yelling about something—a deep bellowing voice that reached right down your throat and grabbed you by the guts. He was the only grown-up we knew who cussed openly in front of us. 'Goddamnit, boy,' he'd shout, 'haul your ass in here!' Skippy always had Band-Aids on his arms and welts on his face, he got knocked around pretty good at home.

"Sometimes at night, while we were hiding behind the McDougals' azaleas or crouched in back of Mr. Pantano's Dodge, we'd hear old Dal Wooten hollering at his wife, or Skippy, or at the twins, which his mother had that July. We'd hear things breaking, hear the babies squealing, sometimes we could even hear Skippy bawling."

"Nobody did anything about it?" Lilah said. "Nobody's parents?"

"In those days, everybody minded their own business. Rusty, one of the big kids, you know, twelve or so, he told us to lay off making fun of Skippy.

"But the thing you have to understand, we liked Skippy. He was a great kid. He would do anything, I mean *anything*. He used to play chicken with the freight trains on the B&O tracks! He would dive off on the other side of the tracks, just like in the movies, so you thought he'd gone under the wheels, but no, he popped right up like a little, grinning Bobo doll, ready for the next train. We used to see hoboes back there, black men mostly, walking up the tracks. We'd come across their dead campfires."

"Did they carry their bindles slung on sticks?" Lilah asked.

"No, they mostly carried paper sacks. Sometimes they came to the back door, and my mother would give them day-old bread or freezer-burned, old meat, let them drink out of the garden hose.

"Come August, the nights were getting colder. One day we found a clutch of baby rabbits out in the woods. It was in a part of the woods where we didn't often go because it was too boggy. Spooky, you know—vines hanging down and thick putrid smells. The whole bog was one big ghost story—they used to say the hoboes hid back in there and roasted little kids."

Lilah said, "Your parents just told you that to keep you the hell out of there."

"Didn't work, did it?" Mike observed.

Nobody ever lets you tell a whole story on through. "There were snakes, too, big copperheads. I don't know what we were doing in the bog that day, but we pushed aside the briars, and there they were—three baby rabbits, dead, stiff as can be, frozen to death. But all nestled together, peaceful looking, like they were only asleep. Skippy was fascinated. He petted them a while. We wanted to take them home, but Skippy said leave them be, so we did. He tucked ferns around them and put up a little cross."

I needed more wine if I was going to finish this, so I gulped what I had left and poured a generous glass. Mike helped himself, and Lilah got up to lay another log on the fire. Maeve nursed her wine, hands wrapped around the glass like she was warming them.

"We'd built a really nifty fort out in the woods. Dug a hole at the base of a big oak and framed logs over it, then piled brush over that. Dragged in some broken furniture and an old throw rug out of the trash and used to go there and read comic books and drink Cokes.

"One day, we were all hunkered in there having a good time, when here comes Dal Wooten bellowing down the path. Before we can get away, he shoves his head into the doorway of our fort. 'Goddamnit, boy, haul your ass out here!' he hollers, and Skippy scutters out.

"Old Dal has the leg-brace in his fist, and he whups Skippy right across the face with it, knocking him down. He hauls him up by the neck of his t-shirt, ripping it, and whales on him some more.

Skippy, he's bleeding and bawling, but we don't dare interfere. We hide inside the fort, pissing ourselves. He beats that boy all the way home, and after they get home, he beats him some more. Then he beats his wife so bad the cops show up, and Dal spends a couple of weeks in jail."

Telling about it, I could smell the damp innards of that fort, the sweet aroma of crow's feet spread over the dirt floor gone rank with our piss. Feel the pulpy weight of the comic books, taste the flat coke rising in the back of my gorge, see that big red hand swinging steel and leather against that little, twisted kid. Then, later, how it felt to stand with my parents in the gathering chill of an August evening and watch the two policemen lead Dal Wooten out to the prowl car, hands clipped behind his back, everybody in the house crying.

"Skippy didn't come out of the house for a couple of days. It rained a lot anyway, and we messed around in Gary Jameson's garage instead of at the fort. By and by Skippy shows up—with two black eyes, a swollen ear, and a short-arm cast, but spunky as ever."

"Wasn't he afraid of what would happen when his stepfather came back?"

"All he said was, he knew how to fix that faggot good. We called everybody faggot in those days, it didn't mean anything."

"Fix him?" Lilah said. "Meaning what, exactly?"

"He never said. Maybe he was just talking." The Jamesons had a pinball machine in their garage, and we'd open the garage door to feel like we were outside and have a tournament all day long. Skippy won a lot, and when he won he giggled, and we liked it that he won. I remember that. At noon he'd pull a mushed peanut butter sandwich out of his pocket, or Gary's mother would bring us all noodle soup and Kool-Aid.

"At night, it would clear up and we'd play kick-the-can under the streetlight, and for the first time Skippy started staying out with us. He was a terrific player—he could hide anywhere, right in front of your face. He'd hide under cars and in trees or mold himself in back of the McDougals' lawn jockey. Once, while I was hiding my eyes and counting to a hundred, he shimmied right up the streetlight pole, and after I had hunted down the others, came sliding down like a fireman and kicked the can.

"I could still hear the can whanging up the street into the darkness, the kids scattering, Skippy giggling and hooting and melting into the shadows across the street, moving silent and fast. Nobody called him to come home. We all drifted off one by one, and left him there by himself under the streetlight—he didn't care. Sometimes I watch him for an hour from my window. He'd just sit there, winging pebbles into the street. Once I saw him head off into the woods, a crazy thing to do at that hour.

"The very next day, two hoboes came to our back door. Big men, grimy and sullen. My mother gave them sandwiches and a jar of iced tea, and they stole two of my father's best shirts off the clothesline.

"A few days later, the cops brought Dal Wooten back, and something was wrong. It was the first day of school, so I didn't know anything was up until late in the afternoon. Skippy had not been on the bus, but then he missed a lot of school, so it didn't seem unusual."

"But he was missing," Maeve said, like she knew this story.

"Let me tell it," I said, but gently, and, I don't know why, I touched her arm, the way you do sometimes to your wife. Lilah noticed but didn't say anything. Mike was pouring more wine.

"Skippy was gone. But it was worse than that—I could tell, because Dal Wooten was sitting on the front stoop with his head in his hands, crying like his heart would bust." Of all the remarkable things that came to light that day, in some ways that was the most remarkable of all.

I paused to let them wonder a moment and we all listened to the fire snap and hiss.

"What happened?" Lilah finally said.

"His wife. Somebody cut her throat. She'd been dead for days. I overheard my father talking to the other men in the neighborhood."

"Christ," Mike said.

"And the babies were gone."

"My God," Lilah said. "Where was Skippy?"

"They looked for him all over town. I took the cops back to our fort, where I hadn't been since the rains had started. It was all caved in. They rooted around in the mud and logs and brush and didn't find anything but a few old comic books and a mess of Coke bottles."

"They never found the kid or the babies?"

"All the men in the neighborhood went on a search party. They found his leg-brace by the railroad tracks—all mangled. Run over by a train, they figured, but there was no blood. They guessed he had hopped a freight, but I didn't think so."

"Why not?" Mike said.

"It was a flat, straight track, the trains rocketed through there full speed. No way he could get aboard. That's why we'd see the hoboes walking—they would get off other trains at the Chrysler plant and hike up the line past the trestle, to the division, where they made up the new trains. Two miles or so."

"He could have gone up the line," Pat said.

"That was the second theory. The cops rousted out the whole hobo jungle, but nobody had seen a skinny kid. They did run across two tramps wearing brand-new Arrow shirts, one of them all bloodstained."

"Your father's," Maeve said.

"Right. Laundry tags sewn inside the collars."

"So they were the culprits," Mike guessed. "The mysterious strangers."

Lilah swigged her wine to the bottom. "Actions never lie."

"Apparently," I said. "The police pulled them in, and it wasn't long before one of them turned his buddy. Signed a statement that said the other fellow had cut her throat and they'd both rifled the house."

"Any evidence?" Lilah said.

"The bloodstains. And they had too much money, could have come from the house. Dal Wooten never used a bank."

"But what about the twins?" Maeve said. She wasn't drinking anymore.

I sipped my wine. "Who knows? They never said. They never admitted anything. Said they never even saw Skippy."

Pat said, "I hope they fried them both."

"The one who confessed was convicted as an accessory. He died of tuberculosis after a year or so in prison. The other guy got the electric chair."

"For real?" Mike said, as if it were the coolest thing he'd ever heard.

"For real."

"Guilty?" Lilah said.

"He never admitted anything. Said he got the bloodstains in a fight over a card game. After a while, the search for Skippy and the twins was called off. Dal started drinking hard and lost his garage. A year or so later he went into a public toilet and shot himself."

Lilah said, "And why are you telling us all this now?" The fire was guttering in the grate, and I couldn't bring myself to get up and throw on another log. Outside a sleeting rain had started, and the rivulets froze in thin lines on the outside of the picture window.

"The other day, my father sent me a newspaper clipping in the mail. They were finally clearing that woods for a subdivision, and they ran across human remains. Bones. I called him up and he told me the details."

Maeve was watching the sleet, her hands folded gently on the small rise of her belly. Her blond hair fell softly around her flushed face. She was due in late spring. Mike had his head in his hands, listening, but he looked tuned out. He was a sleepy drunk.

"Skippy," Lilah said, always so sure of herself.

"No, infant bones. The twins. They were clearing out the bog and stopped for lunch, and one of the workmen noticed a part of a skull."

"So the hoboes buried them in the woods," Lilah said.

Maeve said, with a certainty of her own, "Maybe not. Maybe Skippy."

Lilah said, "Whyever would he do that?"

Maeve said, so softly I almost didn't hear, "To save them."

I nodded. But for the past few days I had been trying to decide: save them from the hoboes, or from Dal? Could he have done that to his own mother, or was he, too, just a victim? And if he did it, he killed that hobo, too, just as surely as if he'd pulled the switch himself. And he might as well have stuck the pistol in his stepfather's mouth. Or else he didn't do any of it, and the hoboes really were guilty.

Nobody spoke for a while. The room felt suddenly chilly. Maeve was sobbing softly. Mike was annoyed with her, and when he tried to put his hand on her shoulder she turned away. "It's the hormones," he apologized. "You know how they get in that condition. She's not even supposed to be drinking wine." He patted Maeve anyway. "There, there, honey."

Lilah said, "But then what about Skippy? Where did he go?"

How could I explain it to her? I remembered the last night I'd ever seen him: loping crookedly off into the woods, melting into the darkness, leg brace swinging from his left hand, white cast flashing above his right. A skinny, dumb, happy-go-lucky, broken kid, who went into the woods and never came out.

What could I say to my wife, who believed that all human action can be accounted for?

How could I make her understand that he had never had a chance, that where he went was the swampy woods where his imagination lived, where wild things nested peacefully, even in death, where a homemade log fort could hide you, but only until they came looking, where the racket of trains was a cause for joy every morning and heartbreak every night, where the hoboes lurked among their smoking cook fires and left behind ghosts that crowded your dreams for a lifetime?

That childhood is a dangerous country, and not all of us make it out alive?

Philip Gerard is the author of four novels and seven books of nonfiction, most recently *The Art of Creative Research—A Field Guide for Writers* and the novel *The Dark of the Island*. He teaches in the Department of Creative Writing at the University of North Carolina Wilmington.

DARK BRAID

This exceptional debut from Dara Elerath enthralls readers from the first poem and reminds us: "This is why I endanger myself." We live and read with the hope of encountering such deft lyricism, to remain with the collection's speakers from imperative through disclosure. *Dark Braid* coruscates linguistically, whether we follow the lines down the page through rhyme and sonic turn or through sinuous prose poem lines. Celebrate this book, one of the most compelling new works from graduates of the Institute of American Indian Arts.

—Joan Naviyuk Kane, *Sublingual*

Dark Braid, Dara Elerath's first book of poems, leads the reader into parallel worlds where beauty exists alongside the grotesque; animals, flowers, and food sit alongside death. Like dripping jewels, each of Elerath's poems is a glimmering collage of images clipped from anatomy and botany books, old Grimm Brothers' fairy tales and from the pages of fashion magazines. Mythic, and yet grounded in the contemporary, these masterful poems are delightful: a surprising and exquisite poetry collection.

—Cynthia Cruz, *Guidebooks for the Dead*

DARK BRAID

poems

Dara Yen Elerath

Winner of the John Ciardi Prize for Poetry
Selected by Doug Ramspeck

BkMk Press
University of Missouri-Kansas City
www.bkmkpress.org

BkMk Press
University of Missouri-Kansas City
5101 Rockhill Road
Kansas City, MO 64110

Executive Editor: Christie Hodgen
Managing Editor: Ben Furnish
Assistant Managing Editor: Cynthia Beard

**Missouri
Arts Council**
The State of the Arts

Partial support for this project has been provided by the Missouri
Arts Council, a state agency.

See page 85 for a complete list of donors to BkMk Press.

Library of Congress Cataloging-in-Publication Data

Names: Elerath, Dara Yen, 1978- author.
Title: Dark braid : poems / Dara Yen Elerath.
Description: Kansas City, MO : BkMk Press, University of Missouri-Kansas
    City, [2020] | "Winner of the John Ciardi Prize for Poetry selected by
    Doug Ramspeck." | Summary: "Through the use of imagination, fairy tale
    and persona, the poems in Dark Braid bridges the universal and the
    personal by focusing on the body, problematic relationships, illness
    (both mental and physical) and feelings of being an outsider"-- Provided
    by publisher.
Identifiers: LCCN 2020040910 | ISBN 9781943491278 (trade paperback)
Subjects:
Classification: LCC PS3605.L383 D37 2020 | DDC 811/.6--dc23
LC record available at https://lccn.loc.gov/2020040910

ISBN: 978-1-943491-27-8

This book is set in ITC Korinna and Acumin.

ACKNOWLEDGMENTS

Grateful acknowledgment is made to the following journals, in which versions of these poems first appeared:

AGNI: "The Museum: Woman with Apple," "The Museum: The Ashtray"

The American Poetry Review: "The Potato," "How to Mount a Butterfly," "Via Dolorosa," "The Sick Man," "The Breasts," "How and When to Use an Eraser," "Mathilda's Testimony," "Saint Pain"

Poet Lore: "The Disappointment of the Cantaloupes"

Wildness: "The Book of V.," "How He Achieved Pure Perception"

The Los Angeles Review: "Hansel and Gretel in Reverse"

Superstition Review: "{ }," "The Blackberries"

Plume: "Testimony of an Armless Man"

Diode Poetry Journal: "The Lyre," "The History of my Body"

Boulevard: "Draw"

I am deeply indebted to Aaron Barreras for his tireless dedication to fostering my writing; without him this book would not exist. I also wish to acknowledge those who mentored and encouraged me throughout my MFA at the Institute of American Indian Arts, including Sherwin Bitsui, Jon Davis, Natalie Diaz, Santee Fraizer, Joan Kane, Dana Levin and Ken White.

I offer my heartfelt thanks to Mikki Arnoff, Chandra Bales, Amy Beeder, Naoko Fujimoto, Brea Gable, Beth Lee, Kristina Marie-Darling, Matthew Pridham, the students, faculty and staff at IAIA, and all those whose friendship, support and feedback helped to bring this book into being. For his inspiration and insight I give thanks to Orlando White. Finally, I extend my deepest gratitude to Doug Ramspeck and BkMk Press for believing in my poetry and venturing to publish this collection.

For my parents

CONTENTS

Foreword   9

I

How to Mount a Butterfly   13
The Book of Joshua   14
Dictionary   15
The Lyre   17
Draw   18
Saint Pain   20
The Name   21
Hansel and Gretel in Reverse   22
The Lesson   23
Blackberries   25
The Followers of Saint Strawberry   26
Ode to the Tongue   28

II

The Disappointment of the Cantaloupes   33
When I Was a Garden Spider   34
The History of My Body   37
Mathilda's Testimony   39
Toad's Confession   40
The Potato   42
Ugly One   43
Undressing   44
Augury of Snow   45
On the Transformation of a Woman into a Frog   47
The Museum: Woman with Apple   48
Diving Bell Spider   49

III

The Hands   53
The Sick Man   54

Via Dolorosa   55
The Faulty Eye   57
The Survival of My Wound   58
Testimony of an Armless Man   59
How He Achieved Pure Perception   60
The Museum: Ashtray   61
The Museum: Salt   62
Speech Delivered on the Terminus of the Glacier   64

IV
Radish   69
The Secret Told by the Cantaloupes   70
Sweat   71
The Dolls Explain Themselves   72
Epistle from a Poppy to a Cactus   74
Hatred of the Moon   75
Violence Against Apples   76
The Pencil   77
{ }   79
The Book of V.   80
How and When to Use an Eraser   81

Note   82

FOREWORD

In *Dark Braid*, Dara Yen Elerath's dark and disturbing debut collection, the poet crafts fables for the body. In "The Survival of My Wound," she writes:

> Will you tend me, my wound asks, as you tend your garden?

With a scrupulous eye for the body's frailties, the poet crafts urgent and eloquent elegies and autopsies, the scalpel of her language exposing bone. In poem after poem, Elerath chronicles in spare and suggestive narratives the fairy tales of living inside the confines of skin, and exposes the feral underbelly of personal myth.

Here, then, are the geographies of grief and wonder as told by bodily loss: exchanged hands, faulty eyes, missing arms. There are poems about tongues and the flesh's decay. Food appears in parables of the self: potatoes, radishes, cantaloupes. And the speakers find metaphors for identity in the natural world, imagining themselves as spiders, glaciers, moons, cacti, poppies, and amphibians. So, too, artifacts and myths and fairy tales serve as stand-ins for the personal, including in one particularly affecting poem, "Hansel and Gretel in Reverse." The story is told backwards, and so we end with the pair finding themselves missing the witch and the way "her knuckles rapped our knees as she appraised our bodies, turning them back and forth to check the fat; this, a thing that every loving mother does."

What makes these poems so engaging is the way the poet constructs them from contradictory elements. The works feel both personal and mythic, existing in some liminal seam between fable and confession, mingling in complex and surprising ways the public and private. Elerath is a lexicographer of the flesh, and the primitive mood she creates is both sensual and dreamlike, the texture often playful and serious in the same breath, evoking with dark humor a human landscape that simultaneously inspires and appalls.

The cliché is that "time heals all wounds," but Elerath is less sure, seeming more inclined toward Kazuo Ishiguro's statement in the *The Buried Giant*: "How can old wounds heal while maggots linger so richly?"

The voice across these superb poems summons us to the body's calamities. In "the Secret Told by the Cantaloupes," Elerath writes:

> I'm done. I want no more
> of beauty. Let me be rank and rotten,
> let me give off the odor that repels.

Yet in the music of *Dark Braid*—in clear-eyed examinations of the estrangement of the self—Elerath arrives again and again at unlikely beauty.

—Doug Ramspeck

I

HOW TO MOUNT A BUTTERFLY

Be sure to hold her wings
between thumb and forefinger;
this will take practice.
Imagine tugging the unthreaded hairs
at the nape of a young girl's neck.
It is important to be swift
but firm, to brush her rouged cheek
with the back of your calloused hand.
When seducing a beautiful woman
insults make the best openers.
Mention mascara blackening
the rim of her lower eyelid,
or complain about the lace
fraying at the hem of her skirt,
the way she blinks too frequently
at neon lights that glow
through the bar's
smoke-darkened windows.
Place her in the relaxing jar.
Alcohol provides another way
to soften her resolve.
If a woman wears a satin dress
she wants you to imagine her
with golden orchids on her breasts;
of all flowers, orchids
are best at resembling insects
they want to attract.
Last, attach her body
to the mounting board
with a silver pin.
Lepidoptery is a hobby
often pursued by intelligent men.

THE BOOK OF JOSHUA

To be loved is to lie in an unmade bed
while Joshua looks on
stroking a handful of Jupiter apples.
When he closes his eyes, I disappear.
Entries from the dictionary
pass through my mind—*prognosis*
is the course a disease will take,
while *sleep* is a time of stillness
when we take on the face
of someone dead.
My only symptom is prolonged fever.
When I leave the house I tie
silk thread to the door—
in this way I am Theseus, only
the Minotaur is who I return to,
only Joshua's hands are nowhere near
as soft. Sometimes, when I touch
his shoulders, I recall
how rain tapped my thin anorak
as I stood on the ledge
of St. Johns bridge before I jumped.
When they hauled my body out of the blurred
current the first thing I asked for
was a bloom from a Joshua tree.
His name means savior, or
one who rescues from peril.
This is why I endanger myself.
Just now, for instance, I have cut
the tip of my right thumb,
but Joshua is nowhere in sight.
I am gathering all the red
like a length of taffeta ribbon—
I'm putting it in a basket to give to him.

DICTIONARY

I have gathered them for you,
these words you touch now,
searching for the meaning
of *fear: a passing emotion
related to harm or danger.*
You recite my entries
as though they were prayers,
caress my pages as you would
a psalm book's, a breviary's.
I am always careful
to use precise language:
*tooth is a structure
in the jaws used for chewing.*
I do not mention
the way it breaks, tears flesh.
I am balm for a *wound:
something that hurts one's feelings,
or a cut inflicted by force.*
When I speak of pain I do not say
forever, when I speak of sex
I do not say *addiction, mystery.*
My sheets are creased,
stained from times
you've stroked them in the bath,
hungry for definition—
the way your *body* is contained
by the tub, the way it is defined:
*the physical form
of a person or creature.*
The way *creature* is used
to describe something wild.
Turning my pages, you find

the word *tame*. Rolling
the letters over your tongue,
you recite your spell:
to make less powerful,
to control.

THE LYRE

My husband asks forgiveness. I say yes, always yes. When he bends his head I think of unction, the act of anointing a man king with holy oil. Long ago I anointed him. I was his queen but time proved me less than a vassal. I poured his ale into a wooden vessel as he pressed his lips against the neck of another woman. I skimmed the thickening skin from his evening milk. I embraced him and he dragged my body across a grass-thick field. I began to think I was an ox. I believed my only purpose was to haul water. I believed that if I faltered it was his right to flog me. When I wasn't an animal I was a baker raising a loaf for him, I was a huntsman thrusting a spear in the heart of a boar for him, I was a shoemaker smoothing and burnishing the leather of his boots. I was a whole village for my husband. I knew he was a great man with many needs. I felt how my knees had grown raw from appeasing him; yet, I commended myself on being a good wife. Sometimes, I would query the night, sometimes, I would peer into a dark scrying glass; sometimes, I would lie in bed and wait for him to come home. Now I know a woman can become a stone for her husband to trouble between his palms, now I know a woman's bones can bend to form a hammer, a nail, a scythe—any tool her husband desires; now I know she can be bound with wire, carved into a lyre, locked in a closet; now I know she may come out only when she is to sing. Now I know my wedding ring is the head of a tuning peg. When he tightens it I scream higher.

DRAW

Do not draw his name
in the margins of your notebook.
Sketch the other woman,
her head resting
in the dark prayer of his palms.
Watch the wildlife show—
whales drawing trails
of pale foam behind them.
Study the way they mate,
in slow motion
under blurred blue, brine flowing
through their open mouths.
Five hundred feet
beneath the sea's surface
love must be weighted,
you think, but know the truth—
whales are not faithful,
they stray to other pods
in search of other bodies.
Stay where you belong:
in the bedroom.
Think of the word *draw*,
how it means, also, *to drag*.
Desire, for example,
drags to an end, yet you must
remain together. This
is called *monogamy*.
Parasites marry
their hosts, as well, consider
the horsehair worm,
Nematomorpha, the way
it penetrates the cricket,

the way it grows,
steadily, inside. When it senses
the presence of water
it whispers to the insect:
if you love me, give
yourself up.
If you love me, it says, *jump.*

SAINT PAIN

It is snowing when he comes to my door. I let him in and feel his fingers trace my sacrum, slide suddenly up the knuckles of my spine. "A year of sorrows if you take your hand off the back of my neck," I say. He leans close to my ear, lips pressed to my cheek. "Have you forgotten the other barters you've made—five years of ache to be free of fear, six years of loneliness to be clear of doubt?" The air in my room is still, filled only with the breath of moths, the brush of his footsteps along pinewood boards. He says he will visit more often now. He stands in the bathroom combing lavender oil through his hair, an artist who knows how to thumb my collarbones, how to touch the fine tissues in my wrists. He returns to me each morning, each evening. Soon, I start to dream of his city, its prisons and wardens, the dust motes that travel through shafts of sun, past rusted bars. I begin to picture a life together, how I will write him notes on stone tablets, how he will read them nodding, touching the letters, mouthing each word like a kiss.

THE NAME

Each time I fell in love, I was given a new name. Numerous suitors came to my town and thus I collected many. On my sixtieth birthday, my last lover died. His temper had been cruel, so I did not grieve, yet I was forced to bear the name he'd left me: *Invisible One.*

Once, on a cold, moonlit night, I wove my silver hair in braids and followed a hidden path to the river. There, I met a monk in a black cowl and told him my story. When I asked for help he said nothing—wind whipped the hempen cord of his cloak. He pulled a stained matchbook from his torn sleeve and wrote in swift, unbroken script:

Touch the stones, daughter—it is winter.

HANSEL AND GRETEL IN REVERSE

When the witch pulled us from the oven, we were beautiful, Hansel. Our hair turned from cinders to flaxen strands. Our skin thickened, sweaters knitted themselves across our chests, wooden shoes cooled and hardened on our feet. Yet, we had to leave that house of gingerbread and licorice. We stumbled backward through the forest, pained to see the witch's face grow distant. Brother, do you remember? Breadcrumbs flew up to your palms like birds. They formed a loaf of sourdough round and thick as the moon. *Mother*, I heard you scream as we blundered blindly through night-thickets, through cracked ribs of trees. Now, in this new house, with this new family, our bodies grow smaller. Hansel, what enchantment have they wrought on us? At dinner, the woodcutter pulls blood sausage from his lips, and the wife turns it into a pig. I fear she is preparing us for something. Note the delight she takes in brushing dirt onto our faces, in removing clothes from our bodies and placing them in oaken drawers. Between her legs there is the scent of something terrible, the scent of a graveyard. At night, in my dreams, I still hear the buckle of the witch's belt clattering, that rattle of our infancy. Brother, let's go back. I miss the cage and flame, the witch's palms stained with ash, the way her knuckles rapped our knees as she appraised our bodies, turning them back and forth to check the fat; this, a thing that every loving mother does.

THE LESSON

A girl holds a paper heart
against a window,
a symbol of something
she's begun to feel.
There is a wheel and inside that wheel
another one. These are the gears,
her mother says, *of the mechanism;*
this is how you wind it.
If it sounds like crying, it likely is.
One's desire is to stay alone,
to withdraw from that unending
hunger to be touched.
To be touched is to be small,
which she already is.
She removes the valentine
from the window,
its color that of muscle, of blood.
She's listening for the sound
of her name, those syllables
she's begun to understand.
Now, the anatomy books,
her mother gestures,
here's the hole where money
goes in, and out of the mouth
come admissions of love, it's like
a fortune-telling machine,
this is how you keep it clean;
the girl lifts her dress
to see the strange device.

What can she glean,
after all, from her body,
she wants to know.

To watch pornography
is to watch animals
rub themselves
to exhaustion.
Something is lost, yet sex looks,
to an outside observer,
like the act of wrestling.
This is not discussed.
That is your lesson
for the day. The mother
brushes her hands as if
to dust crumbs from them.
The girl stumbles
to the garden where dark tulips
and orchids glisten—
blooms she calls by names
of fabled princesses
and millers' daughters.
Look, she says, *look*,
with satisfaction,
showing them
her organism.

BLACKBERRIES

Between the night-lustered blackberry shrubs, I could see the girls crying. They caught their tears in copper bowls and poured them over the soil. Soon, the branches grew heavy; and they reached to gather the fat, unusually swollen fruit. Hands and wrists stained by juice, they laughed like nervous butchers; yet, what were they butchering? What were they eating but sweetness? Their lips bore the color of goat's blood and rubies, the tint of old wounds and bruises. Their laughter echoed until all of the berries were gone. Then they grew sad again. I watched this happen each year. Sometimes, that was all I did—watch them. I longed for their strange beauty. When their tears refilled the bowls, thoughts of the black juice haunted me. Even in winter, as frost glazed the orchard, I could still see them. I sought the hue of that dark fruit everywhere.

THE FOLLOWERS OF SAINT STRAWBERRY

When blood first stained
our underwear we prayed
to Saint Strawberry.
To ease our pain we swallowed
strawberries whole,
measured their curves
with calipers and dipped them
between our lips
to practice kissing.
Half-naked on our beds we lay,
rehearsing the lessons
of Saint Strawberry.
Lesson one: the strawberry
is an aggregate fruit, meaning,
not a singular entity,
but a multiplicity of sweetness.
Lesson two: not all objects
that resemble hearts
are hearts. On Sundays
we took long spoons to market
to dig the richest fruits
from the bottom
of the bin; crushing them
against our thighs
we surprised men we seduced,
consecrating them with the juice
of ripe strawberries.
To Saint Strawberry, we cried,
daughter of all sadness,
mother of all joy. Others claimed
we were mad—
loose women who prayed

to the saint of gashed thumbs,
lacerations, and bruised lips.
Yet, we did not listen,
we stayed in our rooms,
recited our lessons:
Lesson three: seeds that catch
in your teeth are the price you pay
for desiring a strawberry.
Lesson four: unlike cherries they carry
no stone to remind us of hardness,
having a single ring
in the middle they are tokens
of openness. Evenings,
we would stroke the strawberry bushes
to hear songs of the cold, red fruit.
Sometimes, we could hear
the dark roots, too—the way
they roiled below us like an ocean
we were drifting on,
though we did not know
where we were going.
Though we did not know
where we were bound.

ODE TO THE TONGUE

The tongue is how you know you're home.
It cannot be loaned or lost.
It is yours, your own anatomy,
the last thing you mourn
before you lose your life, as the tongue
is how you shape the words
forgive me, understand, wonder.
It is a dream your mouth is having—
that of language that angles
through the archway of your throat
around your gums.
You may use the tongue
to uncover the secret alphabet
a lover draws inside you with his own.
The mystery of the tongue
is how it tries to teach, how it struggles
against lips to speak truth.
Yet, it rarely does—the tongue
mumbles often.
You can soften it with water
or alcohol. You can hush it with sorrows.
In sadness the tongue slumbers for days.
Even if honey is placed on the tongue
it shows no hunger, it gives assistance
solely in shaping the *O*
of a sob. The tongue is tied
by thin wires to the heart,
and if the heart stops, so stops the tongue.
Thus, if you number yourself
among the owners of a tongue,
you may number yourself
among the owners of a heart.

If you doubt yourself
you need only listen
to the tongue, how it whispers
the history of your lovers.
The sounds of their names tapped
on backs of your teeth will lull you
to a silence only the tongue provides,
when the hundred-and-one hungers
of the body are listed, given
to the world, and you are empty.

II

THE DISAPPOINTMENT OF
THE CANTALOUPES

Why do cantaloupes wish to resemble the moon
when, after all, they are filled with seeds, with sweet flesh?
When, after all, they grow along the earth and do not partake
of space, the freezing altitudes the moon moves within?
Why are they not content to be as they are: sunset-hued
beneath their grooved rinds? Instead, they admire the moon,
its cold, withholding demeanor, the pocked face that seems
ground from dry bone. The moon is lonely despite its grandeur,
while melons roll in beds of dirt and wish to burn nightly
with the glow of the sun. They are undone by human fingers,
by knives and teeth—not so the moon. The melons linger
in dusky fields, haunted by flies, tied by tangled vines
to soil. They are weighed down by their role: to multiply
themselves, thus to multiply sorrow—giving nourishment
to blackbirds and wolves, to antelope, insects, children.

WHEN I WAS A GARDEN SPIDER

I knew
I would not
be loved,
not like
those other
animals:
horses,
hares,
hummingbirds,
lambs.
There was nothing
soft
about me,
nothing
one could hold.
Touch me
too hard
and my frail
armor
would crack.
I did not feel this
as a lack but rather,
as the condition
of my living.
I had only
one way
of giving
and that
was to make silk.
I was
no teacher,
or if I was
I taught

the value of knots,
of hanging on.
My life
was a labor
of dangling
from silk ropes,
which broke
at times,
and I began again,
mending.
Mine was a life
of mending,
claiming
I did not mind
being nothing more
than an animate speck
of earth,
worth less
than a curse
from God's lips—
and that's
the other thing,
I had
no lips, no means
of speech
or kissing.
Each day
I was surprised
at my survival,
at the arrival
of sun
on my back,
which,

truthfully,
I could hardly feel.
Some days
I took the life
of a fly.
I could hear
him singing, wringing
his miniscule
hands,
ever anxious
for something,
ever
wondering.
I could feel him
quivering
against
my net,
fumbling
against
my hunger.
Numb,
we were, as all
insects are.
We trembled
together on the web.

THE HISTORY OF MY BODY

I have given up the act
of kissing. It is a task
most taxing and involves
tongues and the passing
of saliva, which calls to mind
the motions of the sea—
motions too unseemly
to be described.
Look, here is a box
of lips I meant to use
before I learned the frisson
between lovers
is a myth meant only
to sell lotion and perfume.
Excuse me please
while I button
this blouse wherein
I keep my breasts.
Excuse me while I close
this drawer between my legs.
Here is the history of my body
in three parts: I was born;
I wore a red dress;
I was not caressed.
Moreover, there is a law that states
no body may touch another
without crushing to death
a handful of innocent cells,
and who can find this
desirable? Better it is
to preserve the body.
Take for instance,

this doll made
to depict human beauty.
See how placid
the painted eyes, how
her hands lie perfected,
prayerful in her lap—
is this not something
to be admired?
How often
I have laid myself beneath
the cellophane sheathing,
folded the bell
of my dress
into the sides
of the cardboard box;
how often I have lain here
awaiting the rapture
stricken on her face.

MATHILDA'S TESTIMONY

My mother kept me in a box. During months of worry she took me out to comb my unwashed hair. She fed me oatmeal, dry bread, and apples, then put me back inside the box. I slept in the box, woke in the box; the scent of oak shavings and amber clung to my limbs. One year she brushed my hair so often that by December there was none left; she rubbed the skin of my ears with oil-slicked thumbs. The more I grew the harder she worked to shove me back in the box. She folded my body like bed linen, like a dress of muslin with glass buttons. Eventually, my spine grew knotted, grew into the shape of the box. Time passed and she died. A family found me; by then I could neither walk nor crawl. One day their youngest daughter put a spoon in my hands and lifted it to my lips. *This is how you feed yourself,* she said. *This is rice and almond milk. This is honey and butter. This is the bone meal they sprinkle on roses to make them grow. This is how you hold a pen. These are the letters of the alphabet. This is your name: Mathilda.* The word sounded strange to me, a blessing I could barely speak.

TOAD'S CONFESSION

Once, I was stone, but some god
gave me these feet, these legs.
Now I leap damp grass
and wade pools of gloomy water,
my back riddled with bumps,
with swollen wounds. At night
I look up at the moon,
which, too, resembles me—
for I recall how, as stone,
I held darkness like a fist
holds the shadow of a palm.
Now awake, burdened with eyes
that drink light, I am afraid.
Sometimes I huddle in gravel,
and none can tell the difference
between my lumpish body
and a cluster of mud, of leaf mold.
I confess I'm most at home
when only the fluttering
of my lungs gives me away,
my need for air, for oxygen.
Truth is, air is thin while dust
is easy to gather. How often
I want to go back there,
to forsake these limbs,
this dumb, ugly mouth,
to crouch down
in muck, in the bad luck
of gnarled roots, pill bugs
and crushed corpses
of spiders. There to be kicked

and licked by winds.
There to be strangled
by moss and washed in night,
unashamed, unseen.

THE POTATO

The potato is afraid of light and movement. It would like to stay hidden forever, fattening slowly in its soft cocoon of soil. Its life is a life of sleep—do not begrudge it this simple existence. It is kin to stone in shape and nature, but softness betrays it. If a worm, seeking moisture, tunnels through, the potato, uneasy, says nothing. Its eyes are scars, they do not shift or lift their lids to note the damage; they do not try to understand. This misshapen lantern dangling from roots has no wish to illuminate anything at all. It is no use unearthing the potato before its time. The vegetable goes slowly. It does not tremble at the pressure of feet aboveground. It does not pray picturing the spade or the farmer's rough, indifferent gloves. Rain falls, sun shines—the potato does not miss these things. Sweetness pours in through its stem, smoothing, straightening the brown paper of its skin.

UGLY ONE

My sister wears glass slippers, they crackle on flagstones at night. Her perfumes fill the house with scents of chestnut roses and snow. She is always quiet, having no need of speech, her beauty its own way of saying *love me*, whereas when I turn my head to catch the gaze of a man, he merely smirks or looks away. Granted, my face is not the kind most desired— yellow teeth crowd my mouth like cowrie shells, my eyes are tiny flies that flicker hunger. Tonight, I lay in the root cellar where squash and pumpkins surround me. Uncomely, lopsided, I find in them kindred forms. The musty air calls back times I'd play with my sister (the other ugly one), how we'd laugh at the weevil's long noses, which, come to think of it, resembled our own. If only I could laugh as I did back then. Now, I finger the skin of an old onion, while through the house I hear my pretty sister bend her skirts like the wings of an angel or a moth pinned to a soft bed. Another suitor. A heel of bread on the nightstand shakes in time to their rapture, its sound that of a hunter running to capture his prey over and over. I hear everything in this underground room. I hear my sister's toes curl, I hear pearls of sweat slide down her slick neck as his thick fingers sleek and plunder her. Sinfully, I touch myself. *Eye of newt and toe of frog*—no spell or recipe will grant me what my sister has. Her long lashes cast down now as if she were bashful, as if she had need of a carriage or fairy godmother. In the streets I hear flea-swarmed dogs plead for porridge or some warm shelter. I cover my mouth so as not to make the same sound.

UNDRESSING

On reaching the edge of the city, you will loosen the veil from your face, remove the knotted cloak you've always worn.

How long it's been, you will think. *Each day I walked from my single apartment, through moon-hazed streets. I have seen many men, though none have seen me.*

Out beyond the neon lights, the rooftops and cars lacquered with rain, you will find silence; having passed your eightieth birthday, you will be fragile, naked, unable to return, knowing if you do they will mistake you for a madwoman. You will realize then all you had was your beauty and you buried it. You will ask yourself if it existed. The trees will sigh in assent, and the saltbrush will ask, *for what purpose?* Grass will simmer at your feet inviting you to lie down. You will think of the carbon particles that compose everything.

I am no different, you will say, *from this dune, these fragments of dry pinewood, these animal bones. I am stone,* you will think, and the sand will scour you. You will be ground down.

AUGURY OF SNOW

Snow falls
outside my window.
It is the greatest
occasion of my life.
I sit in a room
with one bulb burning
above an oak bureau,
and read a book titled:
Ice: A Biography, the story
of a white flake
extinguishing itself
on the sepals of a dying rose.
From that day forth
I dream of drifts
blanketing gray tundra,
powdering a rose;
I picture them
in endless permutations.
Words from the book
enter my sleep: *crystallography,
hexagon, axes
of symmetry, flurry, fog, alp.*
I begin to see
there are letters
etched on each flake;
if I could read them
I would learn
the secret of cold.
As time passes my bones
weaken, a single tear
slips down my cheek.
Sorrow is my first emotion;

it makes me joyful, too.
My heart becomes
a flake of snow,
sad on one side, joyful
on the other. It drifts
downward into the throat
of a rose, like a note
of thanks written
to someone I nearly knew,
someone who stood for years
at the center
of a room they never left.

ON THE TRANSFORMATION OF
A WOMAN INTO A FROG

If, one day, a woman's limbs become frog's limbs, she must find her proper place—underwater, in pond or river. Her lips will blow bubbles filled with pictures from a world she once knew. She will always look to them—glass bottles of amber perfume, a bathroom mirror smeared with soap, a dress of dark fabric, the soft stones of her lover's palms. She will slip through her new habitat with ease, her head soon forgetting her body. She will not sense her skin, how it has cooled, thickened, become ridged like the rind of a lime. She will not see the waterweed stems flickering like fingers beneath her; she will not heed these fingers, beckoning her downward, telling her she's hungry, there are new foods she must eat.

THE MUSEUM: WOMAN WITH APPLE

Come, admire the lambency of bronze
stand on this spot indicated by a black arrow
and note how precise is the engraving
of the human hand holding an apple.
At certain hours the gap between her mouth
and the apple will almost close.
It is through that space,
a distance less than two inches
you can feel the slow hammer of the sea
know the salt-grimed hands of the ocean
as it tries to iron sand to a resting place.
Lean closer and you can hear
the groan of bedsprings in a hotel room
a man breathing in his lover's ear,
her eyes like sudden undercurrents
in hungry waters: drawing him in
and pushing him out again
drawing him in
and pushing him out.

DIVING BELL SPIDER

In spring I anchored my web
in a tangle of eelgrass.
Whatever entered I ate
or mated with.
But tell me, what kind of story
were you expecting?
Before you found me
I had no name, no taxonomy.
Hours passed during which,
if you'd seen me,
you might have mistaken
my stillness for apathy,
for lack of interest.
I've had many thoughts,
the kind animals with eight legs think,
the kind animals who crawl think,
though my crawling took place
in a room two inches wide.
Living in a diving bell
how much can any creature know?
I watched minnows drift past.
In their aluminum armor
saw my fangs, my four sets of eyes.
It was like being visited
by a stranger, my reflection a ghost
who appeared occasionally,
a bit lost, expectant.
I scuttled my net, ate a few fleas,
was not ashamed.
Now, I'm famous, look—
here I am in a guidebook of spiders,
my name: *Argyroneta aquatica.*

You say I'm a wonder of nature,
my life evidence
of divine agency.
You discuss my feeding habits, the markings
on my abdomen.
But have you ever heard my song?
Not a beautiful one, perhaps—
I learned it when I was nameless,
when I did not live
in any textbook, or in the thoughts
of entomologists—
only in my cave of layered silk,
in my undulant bell
of oxygen, of silver air.

III

THE HANDS

I found a pair of hands. Having lost my own to a terrible disease, it was a special occasion. The hands seemed cold so I warmed them with my breath; they were covered in small cuts, so I applied (dexterously, with my mouth) a satin handkerchief. It was the first time I'd encountered such fine, cold hands, such strange, injured hands, and I wanted to prove myself worthy. I asked them to move in with me and eventually, they conceded. I can't tell you the joy I felt watching them lace my shoes, pull the lamp cord at night or scrub Brussels sprouts while I sat at my desk wrapped in a tattered wool cardigan. The disease was taking everything, even my feet and nose, yet those hands wrote letters telling my mother what a wonderful summer I was having. They wrote so many letters I began to believe them. They wrote of the sun, how it shone as I stood in the garden cupping roses, how stones I gathered by the lake were as heavy and bright as gold. I began to think the disease was the best thing that had happened to me. *Those hands rescued me*, I told the priest who came to visit. The fingers—fluttering gently as he stood before me—would reach up to clutch his crucifix; they would fold themselves to pray.

THE SICK MAN

He lay in bed as if struck by a dragon. In the heat of his fever he cried out to God—never before had he cried out to God. Yet, in those grave hours he placed his hands on an altar of herbs, uttered words none had heard before. Each new symptom became a chapter in the book of his pain. One day he was seized with tremor and could no longer hold his spoon. He began to starve. He sought an assembly of nurses to aid him. They became acolytes. He preached illness, a new kind of salvation. He began with breath—*one breath* he'd say, *now another*, and with a rope of air he hauled himself from one day to the next. Then it was water, which he struggled to drink, his throat swollen, so it was *one sip, then another*, and he climbed the rope of water to a plain where fever took him. He lay helpless in a bath of ice; he climbed a rope of fire to get back on his feet. When walking he told himself *one step, then another.* He climbed a rope of earth to a field of level ground. *I've climbed a rope of water, I've climbed a rope of air, I've climbed a rope of flame and sand—I'm ready to be delivered from illness to my destiny.* At that moment, he was struck blind. That was the first sign, they said, of God's divine touch.

VIA DOLOROSA

Somewhere in America, scientists
have invented a method for measuring pain,
running their fingers over the bleach-
burned hands of abandoned housewives.
The standard unit of sorrow
they call a *dol*, as in dolorous, or Dolores,
the name of a young girl skilled
at spilling tears down the buttons
of her cornflower-blue cardigan.
The new machines make us unable
to feign heartache or holy prostration,
but arguments are settled
by those whose dolorimeters run cold.
Some wear the devices against their arms
as a kind of complaint—
this has changed the way we breathe
at 4 A.M. into sweat-soaked pillows
beside breathless bedfellows.
Some sufferers have been sainted,
praised for their ability to hold
their own torn organs in their hands
like blood oranges, the way they tie
barbed wire around their wrists
like penitents hauling wooden crosses
through windless deserts.
It is said if you embrace these men
you will be seared by sudden knowledge,
you will carry the blood clot
of a red poppy in your coat pocket.
When you kiss your lover,
the one leaving a trail of torn letters
in the wake of her battered luggage,

you will turn and say *thank you,*
thank you, and shake
tears from the silver censers
found everywhere these days,
in this strange, fabled country
we can't seem to leave.

THE FAULTY EYE

You will learn to see with your faulty eye, the doctor said. As a girl I tipped my head sideways to take in the view. It gave me the look of mystery, of yearning some ascribed to me, and many came to woo me not knowing I had a faulty eye, that I described the world falsely. On my shelf I kept samples of healthy eyes: round, lucid eyes with pupils poised to take in light, as mine took in only darkness. The larkspur, instead of purple, looked black. When breaking the hull of a nut, I extracted black meat. The blackness was vast, implacable. It ate everything. The faulty eye was a storyteller leaning above a lectern weaving myths. I listened as if listening at the mouth of a twisted nautilus; I heard the drift of sand, crisp as TV static, passing my cheek. Sometimes, the eye would seek waste; it would relish cracked plastic and the ragged shapes of decomposing snails. Later, it would defame my body. I came to hate my breasts and ears, my lips, nose, and thighs. I tried to remove the eye, but it defied me. It weighted my skull like a bowling ball or a burning coal. Like a bullet. Like a stone.

THE SURVIVAL OF MY WOUND

My wound goes to sleep, forgets it is a wound and wanders through a dream of healing. In the dream it sees that to heal is death, thus wakes resolved never to mend. It is caught by the thought of the blade, steel-honed and hard, that carved the hole of its body. It sings to the knife as a nightjar sings to the light of the moon and longs to feel the knife's teeth move, once more, against it. It recites the vows, the tenets of the knife: *to gash, to lacerate, to grind.* The worn, ragged eye of my wound fears it will go blind. *Let me continue to see,* it pleads, *let me continue to be.* I lean above it, marveling at the life I've made. *Will you tend me,* my wound asks, *as you tend your garden?* I watch it thicken, this dark caterpillar resting on the stem of my arm. I touch the clotted blood: thin bristles on the creature's back. I stroke it gently.

TESTIMONY OF AN ARMLESS MAN

I lost my arms in a farming accident but later found I'd grown phantom limbs. There were many things I could no longer do, yet my injury gave me certain gifts. I could caress my wife's phantom breast, for example—the one she'd lost to cancer the previous winter—and brush against my fingertips, from a distance of six thousand miles, the famed Yubari melons of Japan. If a girl in town went missing, I could read her lips by touch and discover her hidden location. Grateful though I was, I longed to hold my own son. Each day I waited to feel him tug my empty sleeve, to climb on the bed and lay beside me. Then, one summer, he died—nothing could console me. Years later I woke with a strange weight in my limbs. *My son*, I whispered, *is it you?* I felt the soft contours of a head shift against my chest and knew I would carry him the rest of my life. No one could talk to me any longer, ask about their absent loved ones or the sweetness of a Japanese melon. Even now as I tell this story I am holding my boy—he is so cold, so silent, his head so heavy against me.

HOW HE ACHIEVED PURE PERCEPTION

The teacher placed the artichoke before him on a small, oak table. *Clear your mind*, she said, *of all but this: the color green, circles of leaves, those apertures you must enter one by one*. Slowly, he moved through layers, felt his way to the spines that hid the heart. His eyes dilated like two caverns that only green entered—green upon green, leaf upon leaf. The teacher offered praise—*You have learned one thing about the world*, she said. *All else will seem a shadow on a screen*. It was true, he had no history but the flower. Soon, each thing he observed he became: a bird in a linden tree, three blue plums on a cold, white dish, a street swollen with cars, a mountain, a building, a city, the world. He could feel the weight of sun as it touched the smallest blade of grass. He trembled to possess so much—yet, when he looked in a mirror he could see each cell of skin, each hair, could see each pore and line. Thus, his face was obliterated. Thus, he ceased to exist. He became instead the air, the wind, the salt of the sea, the earth, a yellow iris twisted in the fingers of a young girl, a red fox, a golden pear.

THE MUSEUM: ASHTRAY

Believe me, it is the most important piece
in our collection. Observe the ashes
floating in gray rainwater—
they are carbon, the basis of all life;
thus, they are the ashes of your grandmother,
your great-grandmother,
and all grandmothers prior.
Here, examine this cigarette end, a replica
of the frayed gold butt you crushed
the first time you made love to your wife
in that highway hotel.
Inside the fine black paper,
grains of tobacco resemble those gathered
in the rambling field your son
will one day stumble through
and are, thus, a symbol of his birth.

When you peer through the ashtray
the world will be different: take,
for example, the couple standing
in front of us examining a found hammer,
note how they seem to blur together.
Imagine it now, imagine space as a ring
notched with swatches of dark matter—
this piece replicates that shape exactly.
It is the sum of all you've been
and will be, your ancestors lining up behind you,
your children fanning out before you,
this clear circle like the first in a series
sent from a stone striking a river.

THE MUSEUM: SALT

The salt in this stone bowl
is uncommon.
It was gathered in baskets
from an ocean
no one remembers.
Taste it and you will feel
your body become synonymous
with salt. The fault lines of earth
will seem to ease open,
causing symptoms
of vertigo, then pain.

Relief is found in offering
the salt to another—
a family member,
so they, too, become afflicted.
You will grow close,
through suffering,
until you are like children
clutching the planks
of a capsized boat.

As you cling to the cracked,
brine-thickened wood
you will realize, suddenly,
how you wanted the world,
how you yearned for it though
there were years you claimed
you did not, years
you filled notebooks
with the names of ghosts
you hoped one day to join.

But I loved my life,
you will cry before
a cold wave rushes up,
before it drags you under.

SPEECH DELIVERED ON THE TERMINUS OF THE GLACIER

Welcome to the glacier.
This milk-white center is the entrance
to the coldest heart on earth.
Eventually, all good things end—
I commend you to the glacier.
You need not wait in the house
of flame nor wade through lakes
of longing. Come straight
to the glacier. Your tears
will turn to snow that falls
in shrouds over shoulders
of lovers who feign indifference
when you enter the room.
Be bold to solder the head
of the adze onto the shaft
of the ice axe, put your back
into the pounding, bear down
to the center of the glacier.
Inside you'll find pure crystal
fists of ice-fruit meant
to flay the skin. What's more
the hands grow numb.
Quit mumbling words of passion
to those who only laugh.
Haul bricks of ice with ropes
and build hereon an igloo.
This place belongs to those of us
who know hope's a disease
spread by bees to flowers
that open, releasing toxins
that cause the eyes

to water. Let's ease ourselves
into the architecture
of the glacier; let's watch now the slow
erasure of earth by frost,
the erasure of that strange,
untameable land filled
with beach sand, pomegranates,
black flies, and boats
lashed to lonely docks.
O please join me
on the glacier, for I have waited here
so long. I see you too
are shivering; believe me
when I say this freezing,
this history of icicle and silence,
this is pure deliverance.

IV

RADISH

You are all I have
to eat tonight.
Your root a thin worm
laying coiled,
hungry on my plate.
I must endure you—
endure the scent of dirt,
the tincture of vinegar
that lingers on you,
the crunch of your body
which is the crunch
of old bones.
How long did you wait
in your home of soil,
communing with ants,
allowing snails
to cross your leaves?
I think of blood
glazing the horn
of a bull who has split
the matador's chest—
this is your color.
Yet, you have not the violence,
the passion of bull fights.
Silent, you hold tightly
to your sulfurs.
When I grind you
between my teeth,
you spill your bitterness
on my tongue.

THE SECRET TOLD BY THE CANTALOUPES

The cantaloupes rot slowly. They sink
down slightly first, then, as if enjoying
their own diminution, they give in.
Deep depressions form in the rinds.
Rivers of mold rise, the melons turn
to planets with forests of hair, with hillocks
of strange grasses. The gasses they give off:
sweet perfume poured over corpses
of dead mice. The melons break as blisters do—
they weep lakes, they summon flies
who come now, numberless, buzzing,
ready to impregnate the meat of melons
with their young. The fruits writhe,
more alive now than before.
No longer bound in the girdles
of their rinds, no longer forced
to bear sweetness, they bear decay,
as if all they wanted to say
was this: *I'm done. I want no more*
of beauty. Let me be rank and rotten,
let me give off the odor that repels.
Each worm and insect stumbling
over the rugged terrain of melons
takes within itself a piece
of their bitter flesh, wanders back
to its burrow or nest. Hereby, the melons
dwell in many countries, they burn
like small flames in the bellies of flies.

SWEAT

The scent of your body after days without bathing
grows to muskmelon long past ripe, its sugars
fermenting to liquor. It is a scent to be drunk on,
a scent of turned earth feathered with flies and woven
with blindworms, the glistening sap of an ironwood tree
slipping down its cut trunk. Though I think, also,
of crushed skunk mingled with marsh flowers,
with humus. Tonight, I ask again that you leave your body be,
that you not erase its scent, which is the scent
of animals racing through your marrow, the hind limbs of lions
and bison arrowing through grass. The scent of your body
long unwashed, seeps across my fingers. I wear it like a ring
and am married to a terrible dark—the larch forest spangled
with spiders, my feet tangled in the draglines of their webs,
the sting of nettles where insects burrow in the dead
flesh of a horse, making there a home, a warm, pungent bed.

THE DOLLS EXPLAIN THEMSELVES

Sometimes you'd trade us
with the neighbor boy,
burn our limbs or cut our heads
right off. At night
your drawers were merely coffins
for our scattered parts.
Yet through it all we smiled
and smiled as no one, not even you,
ever smiled, the whites of our teeth
untarnished for we never ate;
for we gave and gave, even
when you shaved our heads or,
curious, shoved us in the microwave.
All the while you laughed, licking
from your lips the slick sugar
of a candied apple, as if life's sweetness
came in the mangling of flesh.
For how you choked us as you dragged
our naked bodies to your bed.
Though sometimes you held us
as one holds a relic, you listened
at our mouths for secrets,
gave us our names and claimed us,
made us real. So, if now we steal
across your room at night, or seem
to leer from the dresser's edge,
it's just that we began our days
so hoping to impress you,
so hoping to be treated
with a measure of tenderness.
So, if now we seem to thicken
with shadows, our silhouettes

to quiver against the wall, consider:
we are keepsakes of that forgotten
self, that self they taught to become
a woman, that self, that before
the taming, was wild, feral—murder
already stirring in her heart.

EPISTLE FROM A POPPY TO A CACTUS

I do not like you, truthfully. Your spines,
those small teeth, could tear me;
your jade ears are always listening. Your story
of survival is noble, of course, how little
you require, how you break the will
of wolves. Yet, at times I wonder—
would it kill you to be kind?
There are days I long for water,
for what you hide in your hard, green arms.
I have not the skill to coax you, to clear
your thorns. I yield to you, knowing little
of the sun-encumbered plains you grow
so freely on, pushing your roots through rock-
riddled soil. I tally days I've spent
by you, days passed drowsing in this dry,
unsweetened heat. I must be tended
like other blooms: peonies, jasmine, those plants
any hand may gather, weave into wreathes—
those things that do not needle or force
attention, that plead for the affection
of insects, while you traffic with the majesty
of bats, of moths. Next to you I am small, standing
beneath the glowing mouth of the moon,
a reflection of awe at the parched and rim-rocked
ruin of this earth, this poverty that, between
the two of us, you the better have weathered.

HATRED OF THE MOON

Who among us loves the moon? That white,
cratered face peering down, anointing earth
in its anger. Who thought to make myths of him,
that dry specter with his heart of iron, his pitted smile?
At times, the moon is a crown no one wears,
a diadem for emptiness. Nightly, he rolls in his bed
of ice and dust. And what does he dream of
but coming down to touch earth?
What does he want if not to collide with it,
to kiss it like a lustful, limber-fingered lover?
Caught in his net of stars, he envies
most of all the ocean and calls her *whore*—
pregnant, he knows, with drift fish, emperor shrimp,
bones, fins, salt, and scales he cannot
partake of. In jealousy he drags her body screaming
onto shore, batters her over and over—
and we stand here admiring this violence,
we call these beatings tides.

VIOLENCE AGAINST APPLES

Once you bite an apple, it can never be mended; it can never be the smooth, red fruit that rendered its tenderness. Tonight, I watch you slice one. It is not a rattle or a gourd; seeds do not tumble within it like a pod. It is the heart of a god. It is the heart of a man who unclasps his ribcage to hand it to you. What gives you the right to cut it? To destroy it as one destroys something one hates? Is this how you repay sweetness? I watch you gathering apples, clenching them against your chest like pale china, crushing them like tiny skulls. *Crack-crack*, they go, as you ease them between your teeth. Yet, you say something is wrong with me—that I am the one unable to surrender, that I am the one undone by juice and seeds, by thoughts of leaves lusting for rain. You tell me I should step outside my hovel. You shove them before me: *Golden, Gala, Empire, Ginger.* Don't you think I know what comes of eating apples? Don't you think I've seen? The dark seeds roll out like eyes. The core is a bone that's thrown on a heap of other bones. I see your hunger for apples, your taste for sugar and acids. You laugh at me, yet you are the one enslaved to fruit, to gardens and shady orchards—those harems of apples wherein terrible songs are sung. Songs of wonder, of trouble and thunder.

THE PENCIL

A pencil is a useful instrument.
It turns in the black void of the sharpener.
Its tip is licked and applied to a page.
There is no rage in a pencil
unless there is rage in the hand
that grips it. The hand that grips it is slippery
with sweat, red with anger. Perhaps
it is my hand. The pencil has no answer.
It lies on its side like a miniature coffin
filled with lead. How could I ascribe
power to it? How could I look to it
for salvation? The fine striations in the pencil
are beautiful, the ferrule that crimps the eraser
to the wood looks silver but is merely
aluminum, a metal rumored to cause
dementia. The pencil then is sickening.
I do not want it but continue
to hold it. Now, I snap it in half. Now,
I rub the lead across a page so I can crumple
the page to trash. I want
to crumple everything to trash—
the way my husband laughs
as he shoves me on the bed, the way
he hovers as he cuts me down. He calls
the other woman to tell her
he will see her soon, that the blooms
in our garden were grown for her.
Rain stabs the ground like silver pencils.
I hear the sound all night long. I think
how pencil lead lodges beneath skin,
how it leaves a spot that does not
come out, how earth is pocked

with such spots, how you cannot
lie down when covered in wounds,
but lie down you must, as the pencil waits
in its wooden box. The pencil has taught me well.
I mimic the pencil, I get in bed, my husband's head
is still there, its dark hair glistening like the sheen
on letters scribbled by a pencil. I give myself again
to the scent of shavings, to the yellow,
chipped skin of a pencil, to its dreams,
which are dimpled by teeth and nails, greased
by saliva and salt. I give myself to the way
it leans in a bent coffee tin—
beaten, whittled, carved and shaved
past the painted lettering, pressed to the lips
of nervous strangers, forced
to arrange and disarrange language,
forced to say: *I love you, I'll do anything
for you*, when it is only a wooden cylinder
filled with lead. Forced to press
its head to the page and erase,
then write again, only better.
Then erase and write again.

{ }

His two dark arms, wiry as cricket limbs, reach to embrace you. He lives to swallow space yet is never filled. At times you dream he is a gong struck by long-robed nuns, ringing out his single note of *no*. Hours you've devoted to his study. Without knowing, you have sought him in the notches between your ribs, in the pale rings left by a half-spilled glass of milk. He is the hilt on the silver blade of zero; he cuts nothing, yet kills anything that enters him. *Empty set* is what they call him, though *Annihilator* is a better word—he is thoughtless: a black fox hunting in snow, or rotten: a hole in the mouth where a tooth has gone missing. At night he lies beside you, a hollow in your pillow filled with smoke. If you shake a die without pips, his number comes up every time. He is a pair of hips you try to hold. He is a harness which, like a dog, you are caught in, going nowhere, chained to a stake in the ground. The sound of his voice is the sound of wind lifting past you as you choke, as you whimper.

THE BOOK OF V.

Begin on page 49—
find the photograph of female anatomy.
The part that looks like a cut orchid
is a self-enclosed organ.
This is all you need to know.
Seven years elapsed before I was touched
even once, and then it was a stranger
who dropped an envelope in my open lap.
Did I mention his fingers were slick
with Vaseline and I could not bear to look?
His lips were dry and did not carry the scent
of vanilla or Valencia oranges,
did not make any part of my body vibrate.

There are virtually one-hundred-and-one places
to be caressed, but somewhere
between the vertices of the breasts
and collarbones is best (so it says).
Here, I would be remiss
if I did not mention
the virulent strains of kissing disease
featured on page 53.

Tonight, the dress I wore
was viridian, (this might have been
the color of his eyes, had I looked).
There are several versions of the story,
but in the one he told me
Thecla followed Paul to heaven
by never opening her legs;
the only word she wanted
was *vessel*—a porcelain cup rubbed
with white linen.

HOW AND WHEN TO USE AN ERASER

If you've made a mistake while writing a letter to an absent lover, you may consider the advantages of an eraser. It offers the chance to begin anew or to amend those proclamations of undying devotion. The motion of your hand traveling back and forth across the page forms a meditation on the disappearance of your partner. Erasure is a simple skill to master. Practice in your diary by erasing all mention of your lover's name, making space for another. Understand this: the philosopher who discovered the eraser also discovered oxygen. See how the heated rubber peels back the dark spines of the letters to reveal a field of emptiness, how the page opens like a mouth taking air at the end of a kiss. Watch the words turn to crumbs, reminding you of ashes; yet, no ceremony is required to dispose of them. A little residue is always left by the pressure of an eraser. Use the back of your hand to remove it. Tip the paper over the wastebasket. Brush firmly, with quick, deliberate strokes.

NOTE

"Speech Delivered on the Terminus of the Glacier" contains a line from Dean Young's poem "Skipping the Reception."

Dara Yen Elerath's work has appeared in *AGNI, American Poetry Review, Poet Lore*, and elsewhere. She holds an MFA from the Institute of American Indian Arts. She is also a graduate of the Southwest University of Visual Arts and the University of New Mexico. A graphic artist as well as a poet, she lives in Albuquerque, New Mexico. *Dark Braid* is her debut book.

Winners of the John Ciardi Prize for Poetry:

The Resurrection Machine by Steve Gehrke,
selected by Miller Williams

Kentucky Swami by Tim Skeen, selected by Michael Burns

Escape Artist by Terry Blackhawk, selected by Molly Peacock

Fence Line by Curtis Bauer, selected by Christopher Buckley

The Portable Famine by Rane Arroyo, selected by Robin Becker

Wayne's College of Beauty by David Swanger,
selected by Colleen J. McElroy

Airs & Voices by Paula Bonnell, selected by Mark Jarman

Black Tupelo Country by Doug Ramspeck,
selected by Leslie Adrienne Miller

Tongue of War by Tony Barnstone, selected by B. H. Fairchild

Mapmaking by Megan Harlan, selected by Sidney Wade

Secret Wounds by Richard Berlin, selected by Gary Young

Axis Mundi by Karen Holmberg, selected by Lorna Dee Cervantes

Beauty Mark by Suzanne Cleary, selected by Kevin Prufer

Border States by Jane Hoogestraat, selected by Luis J. Rodríguez

One Blackbird at a Time by Wendy Barker,
selected by Alice Friman

The Red Hijab by Bonnie Bolling, selected by H. L. Hix

All That Held Us by Henrietta Goodman, selected by Kate Daniels

Sweet Herbaceous Miracle by Berwyn Moore,
selected by Enid Shomer

Latter Days of Eve by Beverly Burch,
selected by Patricia Spears Jones

Dark Braid by Dara Yen Elerath, selected by Doug Ramspeck

BkMk Press is grateful for the support it has recently received from the following organizations and individuals:

Missouri Arts Council
Miller-Mellor Foundation
Neptune Foundation
Richard J. Stern Foundation for the Arts
Stanley H. Durwood Foundation
William T. Kemper Foundation

Beverly Burch
Jaimee Wriston Colbert
Maija Rhee Devine
Whitney and Mariella Kerr
Carla Klausner
Lorraine M. López
Patricia Cleary Miller
Margot Patterson
Alan Proctor
James Hugo Rifenbark
Roderick and Wyatt Townley

CPSIA information can be obtained
at www.ICGtesting.com
Printed in the USA
JSHW022159290323
39660JS00003B/184

9 781943 491278